AUTUMN'S
COLOURS

MEMOIRS

Cirencester

Published by Memoirs

MEMOIRS
PUBLISHING

25 Market Place, Cirencester, Gloucestershire, GL7 2NX
info@memoirsbooks.co.uk www.memoirspublishing.com

Copyright ©Nick Holloway RGN August 2012

First published in England, August 2012

Book jacket design Ray Lipscombe

ISBN 978-1-909304-05-5

Printed in England

THIS BOOK IS DEDICATED TO:

- My family. Please, when my time finally comes make sure that you choose a decent home.

- West Dorset School of Nursing, Dorset County Hospital, Dorchester, 1972-1975. Thank you for the firm foundation I was able to build on.

- The many wonderful care home staff I've worked with over the years. You've been remarkable people! With just the one exception, you've been a pleasure to work with and I thank you for your friendship.

- Every resident I've cared for. I hope that I was able to make a difference.

- All the care home staff in Dorchester. One of you might be bathing me some day! Somerleigh Court Nursing Home (nice photo of you all on the website) was once part of the old Dorset County Hospital in Dorchester, of course. In my nurse training days it was the maternity unit (of all things!) which meant that it was out of bounds to us male nurses. You may be interested to know that in my nurse training I was actually asked to leave the lecture room when we got to the female reproductive system and get on with some essay writing on my own in the library. No, I'm not joking! Afterwards I asked my female colleagues what it was that I'd missed, and that's how I'm the father of two daughters.

- Kelly Andrews. Thanks for standing by me.

Is my local care home the Golden Halo Care Home? How does it measure up?

Does it deserve a golden halo or to be closed down?

How would I measure up as a carer? I might have the will, but have I got the skill?

Find out in this unique quiz!

Answer the following wide-ranging and probing questions based on Nick Holloway's book Autumn's Colours and then decide which award you would give your local care home:

Absolutely Admirable?

Averagely Average?

Abominably Awful?

Have you got what it takes to be a carer - a good sense of humour, a bit of common sense and a really strong stomach?

INTRODUCTION

When I left school at seventeen I worked as a postman in Bracknell, Berkshire, delivering letters and peddling telegrams. Getting up at four was a bit of a shock after spending my last year in school as a hippy-lifestyle-loving sixth form student.

After my eighteenth birthday in 1972 I left home to start my nurse training at the West Dorset School of Nursing in Dorchester and Weymouth. Wonderful towns, enjoyable times. Qualifying as a State Registered Nurse at my first attempt in 1975, I worked in the operating theatres in Weymouth for a while. I counted all the instruments out and counted all the swabs back. I had a patient with a ruptured aortic aneurysm die on the operating table and my first caesarean section was a dead baby. I bought my first guitar in a second-hand shop in Dorchester high street. I passed my driving test in Weymouth, also at the first attempt. On the whole, happy days.

When my wife, also a Registered Nurse, and I moved to the Rhymney Valley area of South Wales around 1990, I began working in care homes as a Registered Nurse, including five years as a care home manager and some nursing for an agency. After a break of three years working as an NVQ Assessor in the incredible beauty of the Rhondda Valley with 16 and 17 year olds, it was back into care homes. Bored with nursing ('Oh no, not another drug round!') I gained Institute Of Environmental Health certificates and worked in my local care home's kitchen for seven years.

A care home is a care home. A care home in the Rhymney Valley is the same as a care home in Dorset. You wash, you feed, you toilet, you medicate. I imagine that the only difference will be in the level of fees.

I should make it clear that I have never worked in a care home in Dorset. If I can afford it I might retire to Dorchester some day, so I could eventually become a care home resident and experience a déjà vu moment in 'The Return of the Native Care Home.'

Lastly, I pay tribute to the many truly dedicated staff who have worked with me in various care homes over the years. I've enjoyed working with you all and hope that you've enjoyed working with me. Looking after elderly and sometimes confused residents is hard work. From time to time an incident regarding the abuse of care home residents by staff hits the headlines. I have never witnessed any such abuse. I have only seen committed staff working tirelessly for low wages to care for those whom the rest of us either have no facilities or no time to care for. Care home staff are worthy of our admiration! And our thanks.

Nick Holloway RGN

CHAPTER ONE

MAY DAY

Nancy woke with a familiar realisation. There was a warm, wet patch in her bed. She knew what had happened because it happened most nights.

'Blast it!' she murmured. 'Blast it, blast it!'

She sighed and lay there, motionless. After several minutes she thought to press the nurse call button on the end of a long flex that had been wound around the cot-side. A buzzer sounded somewhere in the corridor. She waited for what seemed like ages before she eventually heard footsteps approaching her door. It opened and Pauline, one of the night carers, came in and pressed the illuminated green 'cancel' button over the bed. The buzzing stopped.

'Yes, Nance?'

'I'm wet.'

Without a word the cot-side was lowered, the bedclothes were pulled back and an inspection made. Yes, Nancy was wet. The fact being established, Pauline pressed the buzzer for a few seconds, a prearranged signal, and several moments later one of her colleagues joined her.

'Nancy's wet.'

The old lady was lifted on to the commode next to her bed. Linda lifted the wet nightdress over Nancy's head, took it with the sopping incontinence pad and dropped both on the floor at the top of the stairs. A clean nightdress with the name of a deceased resident crossed out and 'Nance' written on the label was taken from the middle drawer of her wardrobe. Clean sheets were collected from the linen cupboard and the bed remade. It was two-thirty in the morning and very little was said.

'They've been sleeping' thought Nancy. 'I bet they've been sleeping and I've woken them up!'

'Have you had a wee, Nance?'

Nancy wasn't sure what she'd done.

'Have you had a wee?'

'Yes!'

With Linda taking her shoulders and Pauline her feet, Nancy was lifted back into bed. A fresh pad was put in place and the bedclothes pulled up to her chin. The cot-side was raised to prevent the confused old lady from falling out of bed or trying to climb out of it.

'OK?'

'Yes.'

'Off to sleep, then.'

The light was switched off and the door left ajar. As the footsteps receded out of earshot Nancy noticed that the nurse call button hadn't been replaced around the cot-side. It had fallen on the floor.

'Blast it!' she said.

* * * * * *

Pauline, her hands full of wet bedding, nightdress and incontinence pad, began making her way down the stairs. She would dump the bedding and nightdress in the large white canvas bag in the laundry room. The pad would be taken to the sluice room and put into the yellow plastic bag marked 'clinical waste'. The waste contained body fluids of various colours and thickness and would be collected by a licensed company and incinerated.

'I'll do a quick check up here, Paul, and join you downstairs in a minute.'

'Do you want some coffee, Lin?'

'Yes, I'll be there, now.'

Linda, a Registered Nurse, made her way along the first floor corridor, poking her head around the doors, pausing to look around the room and listen for the sound of the occupant breathing. She would go into the rooms of some residents to make a closer inspection, to offer a drink or words of comfort. Some slept with the dim light over the wash-basin left on and others with the main light on. Some slept with no light on at all, just the dim glow from the corridor shining in and casting strange shadows around the room. Some residents slept for long periods, while others hardly slept at all. Some watched the television, regardless of what was showing.

Sleeping tablets were given to a dozen or so residents; they were helpful to some and ineffective for others. A measure of whisky or something similar in a warm drink would often work, but alcohol had to be used with care. It interfered with some medications, either increasing or decreasing their effectiveness.

And then there were those who slept with the door shut, who didn't want or need anyone checking on them during the night. They could press the nurse-call button if they needed something. After all, the leaflet entitled 'An Introduction To The Tranquil Heart Care Home', under the heading 'Philosophy of Care', clearly stated 'every resident is entitled to have their privacy respected'. Unfortunately, many of the staff were not aware that the home *had* a philosophy of care. There was a framed copy of it in the entrance foyer, but nobody ever read it.

The first floor checked, Linda made her way downstairs and did the same on the ground floor. All seemed to be peaceful for the moment, so she joined Pauline and Sarah in the lounge.

'There's your coffee, Lin.'

'Thanks.'

'Are either of you watching this?'

'No, turn it over if you want. It's about time we had Sky put in. Don't you think, Paul? Don't you think the Hindmarshes could afford to put satellite TV in?'

The comment was not lost on Pauline. Linda settled back into the armchair and pulled the blanket up to her shoulders.

'I'm froze! Don't it go cold when the heating goes off!'

* * * * * *

It had been an uneventful night at the home. Those residents who usually slept well had slept well and those who didn't hadn't. Those who were usually wet or dirty had been wet or dirty. Nobody had died and nobody had fallen out of bed, so the Death Book and the Accident Book remained safe and snug in their filing cabinet. The uneventful nights at the Incontinental Care Home were the best ones.

When the long-awaited hour of eight o'clock finally arrived, seven residents, four of them in wheelchairs, were sitting in the dining room. The rule was that no resident should be got up before half past six unless there was a good reason. Needless to say, a good reason could always be found. Linda was not unique in having worked in care homes where residents in their eighties and nineties were got up at five in the morning to be bathed or dressed. Of the nearby Riverside Care Home it was said that all thirty residents had to be got up before breakfast. Since breakfast was at eight o'clock it was not difficult to imagine at what time these elderly parents and grandparents were dragged out of bed.

This morning's early risers were at various stages of eating their breakfast. The always bright and cheerful Tony had started his shift in the kitchen at seven.

Pauline stood in the doorway of the office, putting her jacket on. Linda sat behind the desk, pen in one hand, covering a yawn with the other. The night report was in front of her. Sarah sat opposite her, shoulder bag dangling on the floor.

'Is it all right if we go, Lin?'

'Yes, thanks a lot.'

'See you tonight, then.'

'Bye!'

Pauline stepped out into the fresh morning air and pressed the button on her key ring. Indicator lights flashed as the alarm on her dark metallic blue new-registration BMW was deactivated. She would sleep for a couple of hours before going round to the gym for a moderately energetic workout. In her rush to drive off she didn't notice Dave watching her from his first floor cell. Sarah would walk home.

A weary Linda went to the staff room to round up the morning shift for the handover. There wasn't anything of note to mention, but the staff drifted into the office and Linda went mechanically through the list of residents.

'Fine... no problems with her... slept well... also slept well... painkillers given at 2... wet a couple of times... talking to himself... fine... no problem... slept well...'

The report given, she handed the drug keys to Anna Peters, the Deputy Manager, and wearily left for home.

* * * * * *

And so began another day at the home, one of the many of its kind in West Dorset. Able to accommodate forty residents when it was full, it had only thirty five at present. It was rarely full, because residents either became ill and had to be transferred to the hospital or died and had to be collected by the undertaker. The local authority budget was as tight as ever and funding was only available for care home placements if an individual could not be cared for in any other way. It was usually cheaper for an elderly person to be looked after in their own home if this was feasible, and obviously this was where most of them would rather be.

Some care homes were registered for nursing residents and some for residential residents. Some were dual registered and could accept both. Residential residents were expected to look after themselves to a large degree, to be able to wash and dress themselves, be mobile and be continent. Supervision and minimal assistance, at least in theory, were provided. A residential home would often have no Registered Nurse on the payroll and this would be reflected in the lower level of fees charged, around £550 a week. It was of the utmost importance to maintain a high room occupancy level, because an empty room was a waste of space. It earned nothing.

Apart from the Registered Nurses, staff were paid the national minimum wage for day shifts, nightshifts and weekends. It was time and a half all round for bank holidays.

Anna sat behind the untidy office desk and allocated tasks to the carers, who then went off to tackle their assigned duties. The home's diary was open on the desk and Anna dutifully glanced at it.

An attractive twenty-seven year old, Anna Peters had been working at the home for nearly six months. She hadn't worked for a couple of years following the birth of her first child and was anxious to get back into the cut and thrust of the intensive care unit at a nearby hospital. This care home appointment was a stepping stone on her way back. She would be taking some time off to attend training days and hoped to be back among the cardiac monitors, intravenous infusions and respirators by the end of the year.

The diary reminded her that a group of local junior school children would be making another visit to the home after lunch. This time they would be entertaining the residents with May Day songs and dances around the maypole.

'Why do these visits always happen on my shift?' she thought. But Anna knew that most of the residents would thoroughly enjoy the children's visit. Elderly people and young children seemed to get on well together, at least for short periods. These youngsters' visits had become popular with the old folk and were now a regular fixture. Even so, there would be one or two residents who wouldn't enjoy the visit. You meet such people everywhere, including care homes - people who seem determined not to enjoy anything.

It occurred to Anna that Tony might not have been told about the school's visit, so before making her customary tour of the home she made her way to the kitchen to break the good news to him. Orange squash and biscuits were usually provided. The children's previous visit had been just before Easter, when they had worn Easter bonnets which they had made in their classes. Appropriately, each child had been given a cream egg.

* * * * * *

When Joan bustled into room eight she glanced at the figure in the bed to see if it was awake. It was. In fact, Nancy had been awake for some time. A warm wet patch in her bed had woken her up, but she'd been unable to do anything about it. She now had a cold damp patch in her bed.

'Morning Nance! How are we?'

'I'm wet.'

'What's new?'

Nancy was always wet in the mornings. Even if changing her was the last thing the night shift did, she would still be wet before it was time to get up. Nancy liked Joan, probably because she was one of the older members of staff, being fifty-something and looking forward to retirement. Her husband, Arthur, had already retired from his factory work and they had plans to move away to Bridport. Joan had worked at the home since its opening nine years before and had worked as a carer in hospitals for many years before that. She had the ability to truly understand elderly people, a somewhat rare attribute in care homes.

'Ready to get up, Nance?' she asked.

Nancy would have said something if she hadn't been, but she said nothing, so Joan drew back the bed covers and in one practised movement pulled the diminutive Nancy up and swung her thin legs around so that she was sitting on the edge of the bed. The commode was by the bedside and Joan helped Nancy on to it. She ran some warm water into the basin.

'A quick wash, Nance, just to freshen you up' she said.

The warm flannel was quickly wiped over Nancy's face and hands, Joan chatting all the while. The nightdress that had once belonged to someone else was removed and Nancy's chest and back were washed, dried and powdered. Her knickers were pulled up to her knees and her vest, dress and cardigan put on. She didn't wear a bra. Then the stockings and slippers. Stockings or socks were preferred to tights because they made toileting easier. The choice of clothes was Joan's, since it was unlikely that Nancy had the slightest idea what clothes she possessed. The buzzer was pressed and while Joan waited for assistance she put a brush through Nancy's grey hair. Then she rinsed the old lady's dentures.

'Open wide, Nance!' Nancy opened wide.

For some reason she was particular about wearing her watch. Some carers forgot about it or couldn't be bothered to put it on, but not Joan. Whether Nancy ever looked at it nobody knew, but it obviously had some sentimental value for her.

Joan had begun to strip the bed before Zoe answered the buzzer.

'Hi! Need a lift with Nance?'

'Yes, please.'

'Morning Nance. How are you? Sleep well?'

'No, not very well.'

'Ah, never mind. I expect you'll fall asleep in the armchair after breakfast.'

Between them they lifted Nancy off the commode and Joan washed her resident's bottom, dried and powdered it. She arranged the incontinence pad, the first of four allocated to Nancy each twenty-four hours, pulled up her knickers and the two of them sat her in the wheelchair.

'You'll do!' said Joan.

'I'll take her down with me' said Zoe. 'Anything else to go down?'

'No, not yet, thanks.'

While Joan finished making the bed, Nancy was pushed towards the lift. For her, May Day had begun as monotonously as any other day.

* * * * * *

For Maureen Biddlecombe, life was somewhat more interesting. On a Monday she would attend a speech clinic at the nearby Dorset County Hospital, and would set her alarm clock for seven. She was able to wash and dress herself with a minimal amount of help and on clinic days she would apply a little make-up. Tony would ensure that she had her breakfast on time and the Registered Nurse would check that she had her midday medications in her handbag. Maureen would then walk, aided by her stick, gently down the corridor to the entrance foyer. She would find herself a seat and look out of the window for the hospital car that was booked to pick her up at nine-thirty.

At only sixty-four, Maureen was one of the younger residents. She had retired from full-time teaching, but had continued to involve herself in teaching 'literary skills' at evening classes. That was, until her brain haemorrhage or 'stroke'. She had needed emergency hospital treatment that involved delicate surgery to remove a blood clot from somewhere in her brain. The subsequent improvement in her condition had been rapid and sustained. Having nobody to care for her at home and home being a fourth floor flat, she wasn't too averse to moving into a care home, at least as a temporary measure. If all went well she hoped to return home in a couple of months. She was friendly enough towards the staff and other residents, but she was a woman who preferred her own company. An avid reader of classic novels, she remained a faithful listener to radio four.

The residual effects of the stroke had left Maureen with a slight weakness affecting her left arm and leg. She had difficulty in fastening small buttons and lifting some of her heavier books. Despite these restrictions she managed to do much for herself and had regained a near independence. She walked reasonably well with her stick, and though her speech was still affected to a marked degree she was able to make herself understood, even if this sometimes meant repeating herself. It was because her GP believed that her speaking could be further improved that she continued to attend the Monday dysphasia clinic.

The hospital car, a gleaming dark green Audi, would pull into the drive at nine-thirty. Maureen would pick up her handbag and make her way out into the fresh air. The driver was Ray. He would hold the car door open for her as she approached the car and they would exchange warm greetings. He would hold her handbag as she made herself comfortable in the front seat. He would then close the door. The two of them got on well and had become close friends; closer than anyone at the home realised.

* * * * * *

Two lines of school children, about twenty of them in all, dressed in red jumpers, bounced and skipped excitedly along the pavement. Each had a posy of crêpe paper flowers in their hand, put together with characteristic childlike enthusiasm during their craft lesson. The intention was that each posy would be given by its creator to a resident. Miss Graham carried the colourfully-decorated maypole, and when Mrs Brown pressed the doorbell, St Mark's Junior School's policy for 'creating and maintaining meaningful links with the community' swung into action once more.

Anna and her colleagues had done their best. Now, at two-fifteen, most of the residents were seated in the lounge with their chairs against the wall, leaving enough room for the children to perform their singing and dancing. Toileting had been completed and medications had been administered. Joan was left to keep an eye on proceedings, while the rest of the shift went off to the staff room for coffee or out the back for a cigarette. The concert was due to finish at three, the time the afternoon shift started.

It was obvious that Mrs Brown had the situation under control. She oozed confidence and authority.

'If she had not been a schoolteacher, she could have been a very capable nursing home manager' thought Joan.

'On behalf of the children of St Mark's Junior School, we would like to thank you for allowing us to visit you this afternoon' she began. 'The children have been looking forward to coming to see you, haven't you, children?'

'Yes, Mrs Brown.'

'The children have also been very busy, haven't you?'

'Yes, Mrs Brown.'

'They have each been making a little gift for you.' She turned to the youngsters. 'Now, children, would you like to give these ladies and gentlemen their flowers?'

The boys and girls had been standing just inside the door of the lounge. Mrs Brown had been warned that it might be best if they did not sit on the floor. Cautiously at first, the children moved nervously among the residents, each dutifully offering his or her posy of flowers to whichever resident looked least frightening. It took about two minutes for this 'social interaction with the planned outcome of developing interpersonal skills' to be completed. Then the children gathered once more by the door. Adam was particularly happy. He was the envy of his peers, because he had arrived back with a fifty-pence piece in his hand.

The may pole stood in the centre of the room, and the energetic boys and girls hopped and skipped their way through the presentation. Those who were not gifted with the artistry of gracious flowing movement formed the choir and sang as best they could. Mrs Brown conducted the whole show with aplomb, finishing within a minute or so of three o'clock, much to Anna's relief.

Joan stepped forward and thanked the children and their teachers on behalf of the residents, adding that she was sure that they looked forward to the next visit. The children were led to the dining room for their reward, squash and chocolate biscuits. Mrs Brown and Miss Graham were grateful for the pot of tea.

QUIZ

Some suggested answers are in italics.

'Yes, Nance?'

'I'm wet.'

Without a word the cot-side was lowered, the bedclothes were pulled back and an inspection made. Yes, Nancy was wet. The fact being established, Pauline pressed the buzzer for a few seconds, a prearranged signal, and several moments later one of her colleagues joined her.

 'Nancy's wet.'

1. **If you woke up in the middle of the night and found that you had wet yourself, how would you feel about it?**

- *I would feel -*
- *- Embarrassed. What am I going to say to my partner, my parents?*
- *- Worried. Is there something wrong with me?*
- *- Shocked. I can't believe it!*
- *- Panicky. Do I need to see my doctor?*
- *- Puzzled. What's going on?*
- *- Annoyed. Now the mattress is going to smell!*

2. **How might Nancy feel about wetting <u>her</u> bed?**

- *She simply accepts it as part of growing old.*
- *She no longer cares about what she does. This includes wetting her bed.*
- *She feels embarrassed and bad about it, but staff seem to accept it as normal behaviour.*

3. In January 2001 an official report condemned the use of cot-sides. There had been some nasty injuries and a couple of deaths caused by their use or misuse. Do <u>you</u> feel that their use is justified, or do you agree that they should be banned?

- *Your answer.*
- *Although frequently referred to as 'cot-sides' the correct term these days is 'bed-rails'. The word 'cot' is deemed inappropriate when used of adults.*

My opinion is that a risk assessment should be carried out for each resident who needs to use them. Carers should be aware that the misuse of cot-sides may cause injuries. Padded 'bumpers' should be used with them.

4. List <u>all</u> that Joan did for Nancy as she got her up, ready for breakfast.

- *Joan -*
- *Greeted Nancy by name.*
- *Asked her if she wanted to get up.*
- *Sat her on the commode.*
- *Undressed her.*
- *Explained what she was going to do.*
- *Chatted all the while.*
- *Washed her.*
- *Brushed her hair.*
- *Dressed her.*
- *Put her watch on.*
- *Cleaned her dentures.*
- *Put an incontinence pad in place.*
- *Stripped and remade the bed.*
- *Made a visual inspection of Nancy's skin condition.*

'Sleeping tablets were given to a dozen or so residents and proved to be helpful to some and ineffective for others.'

5. One of <u>your</u> residents is unable to sleep tonight. What could be the reason?

- *They're worried about a relative, friend, neighbour or pet.*
- *They're frightened of dying.*
- *They're upset about the death of a friend, relative or another resident.*
- *They have a stomach ache, arthritis pain, toothache.*
- *They're disturbed by noise from another resident's television.*
- *They're hungry or thirsty; too hot or too cold.*
- *The light has not been turned off or left on.*
- *They're spending too much time sleeping during the day.*

6. What are <u>you</u> going to do to help this resident sleep?

- *Find the time to talk to them and ask them why they can't sleep.*
- *Use common sense to ascertain the problem.*
- *Offer words of comfort, a warm drink, paracetamol tablets, to switch the light off or on, fetch another blanket, etc.*
- *Consider if this should be reported to senior staff.*
- *Ask that they be kept occupied during the day.*
- *Consider if a visit from a church minister might be helpful.*

7. What alternatives to sleeping tablets could <u>you</u> suggest for <u>your</u> insomniac residents?

- *A warm, milky drink.*
- *Watching television, listening to the radio or to music.*
- *Tea and toast.*
- *A covered hot water bottle (if allowed).*
- *A drink of whiskey or brandy, possibly in warm milk, after checking with senior staff.*

- *Reading a book, newspaper or magazine.*
- *Doing a crossword puzzle.*

'Elderly people and young children seemed to get on well together, at least for short periods. These youngster's visits had become popular with the old folk and had become a regular feature.'

8. Why do elderly people and young children often get on well together?

- *Your answer.*

9. Why might older people only be able to tolerate young children for short periods?

- *Your answer.*

10. Why would the children have been warned not to sit on the lounge floor?

- *There could be wet patches caused by urine from incontinent or confused residents.*
- *Drinks might have been spilt on the carpet.*

11. In what ways might elderly people in your care home be treated like young children by carers like you and by their own relatives?

- *They are not asked about or involved in decisions being made concerning them, eg the clothes they are going to wear today, the foods they are going to have for lunch.*
- *Childish expressions are used in speaking to them.*
  - 'Stand up for me, there's a good girl!'
- *They're told off when they have done something wrong, such as wet themselves. - 'You dirty boy!'*

- *They're spoken down to or threatened.*
  - *'You don't want me to have to tell your daughter, do you?'*
- *They are given bibs to use at mealtimes.*
- *Their medications are not explained to them.*
- *They are told to 'eat their vegetables'.*
- *'Just one more spoonful for me! There's a good girl!'*
- *They are pushed around the home in a wheelchair when there is no need for this.*

12. Why might you be treating them like young children?

- *They sometimes behave and talk in a similar way to young children.*
- *They make a mess at mealtimes.*
- *They wet and dirty themselves, wear nappies and have to be toileted.*
- *They can't talk and make themselves understood.*
- *It's easier to control them.*
- *They don't object to being treated this way.*

CHAPTER TWO

AN INSPECTOR CALLS

Most of the residents at the Golden Dawn Care Home would be woken, washed, dressed, breakfasted and tableted by eleven o'clock. Some would have endured, or possibly enjoyed, a bath before or after their breakfast in order to comply with the bath rota which was displayed on the office notice board and in the downstairs bathroom. The more dominant carers kept the bath rota under review, Tippexing out and adding names as residents died and fresh faces arrived. The majority of residents didn't have any say when it came to the when, where and by whom of bathing. They were simply told at what time and on what day they would be bathed. They would be bathed by whoever was available.

'Maude, my dear. Hilary has had to rearrange the bath rota and now your bath day is Tuesdays. All right? Not Thursdays any more. Tuesdays!'

It was inconceivable that there could be any plausible reason for Maude to object to this change.

'That's settled, then!'

Residents were bathed at least once a week, more often if incontinence made it necessary. The more sensible residents might be allowed to choose the day and the time of their bath, and if the resident was insistent enough, a bath could be taken when a favourite carer was on duty to do it. But for those robbed of a sound mind, life was different. It was they who were likely to be bathed as early as six o'clock on winter mornings, since they had no idea what the time was.

The time of day was irrelevant to them, anyway. Baths, together with bowel movements, were recorded by ticking the appropriate column in the 'bath and bowel book'. As if this wasn't enough, a comment would have to be made about both matters in the resident's individual care notes hastily completed at the end of each shift.

As eleven chimed, the majority of the residents would be performing according to the script written for them and be sitting in one of the home's three lounges. The likes of Maureen Biddlecombe, Ralph Edwards and their ilk preferred the peace and safety of their own rooms.

A trolley would set off from the kitchen, and its rattle would be heard announcing the arrival of the mid-morning drinks long before it actually appeared in the ground floor lounge. It would be equipped with an assortment of jugs, cups, mugs, beakers, jars and spoons and offer tea, coffee, drinking chocolate or Bovril. On the bottom shelf a Cadbury's Roses tin would be half full of plain biscuits. Chocolate biscuits or Jaffa Cakes would have made a welcome change, but these were only rarely available. This, it was said, was 'because of the diabetics'.

This morning it was Lisa's turn to dispense lukewarm drinks to the fifteen or so residents that occupied this lounge. She adhered to the advice she had been given when she had first started working at the home.

'Don't give no one boiling hot drinks. If one of them spills it and scalds themselves, their family will more than likely sue us. And bang goes any hope of a pay rise!' Thus it was that none of the residents at The Singing Kettle Home for the Aged could ever remember receiving a hot drink. Warm was the best that could be hoped for.

When the ground floor drinks had been distributed, a tray of tea and coffee was taken to the upper lounges. Those who stayed in their own rooms enjoyed a form of room service.

The large television in the lower lounge was on all day and was always on ITV. Any attempt to change the channel was met with immediate protests from Old Rose, the older of the two residents with that name. Old Rose also protested whenever a window was opened, no matter what the time of year.

'I don't care! I want it closed. I'm perished!'

There would be five or six folk in the first-floor lounge. It was a smaller and quieter room than its downstairs equivalent and its television was off more than it was on. Two framed black and white photos of 'Old Dorchester' hung on one of the walls. Like the other lounges, the walls were the same boring magnolia and its chairs were high-backed and made from a blue vinyl that could be washed easily should any mishap occur. The carpet, also blue, was of a special type that was suited to 'environments where urinary incontinence might otherwise be a significant problem.'

The Happy Memories Home for the Elderly had several residents who suffered from various forms of dementia such as Alzheimer's Disease. Some of these folk were good on their feet and presented a considerable risk in regard to their security and safety. They were capable of escaping!

These individuals were taken to the downstairs lounge, where it was easier to keep an eye on them. It was, the Manager said, simply a matter of risk assessment. Despite everyone's best efforts, though, occasionally someone would manage a brief escape, wandering optimistically down the street before being recaptured.

In much the same way as these residents might, in years gone by, have sat as parishioners in the same church pew each Sunday, so most of them now sat in the same armchairs all day. This allowed staff to cast a quick glance around the lounges and guess with reasonable accuracy who might be in the toilet, who might be in their own room and who might be somewhere they shouldn't be. It also presented a problem. Squabbles would occasionally break out because someone was sitting in someone else's armchair.

* * * * * *

Dave didn't say much. Except to himself.

She's coming over to you. You know who she is. She always comes over to you. Never fails to. In a minute. Give her time. The poison woman. The guard with the poison. Here she comes, regular as clockwork. They've sent the pretty one to me this morning, but she won't be on her own. There'll be others. They all work together. Resist, Dave! Be brave, Dave! It's useless to resist them, but you must! None of the others will resist, Dave, but you must. I must resist them. Perhaps the others don't know what is going on, but I do. Don't drink it, Dave! It's poison, Dave. What are you doing, you fool, you're drinking it!

'Finished with your coffee, Dave?' asked Lisa.

'Yes thanks, I have. I've drunk it all, thanks.'

* * * * * *

With the drinks trolley safely back in the kitchen, it was time to toilet those who needed to be. The 'feeders' would be taken to the loo first because they would be the first sitting at lunchtime. The results of this toileting varied, depending upon the administration of diuretic water tablets earlier that morning and opening medicine for the bowels the previous evening. An over-enthusiastic administration of the latter could make the situation on the following day somewhat dire.

'I tell you what, if I don't win the damned Lottery this week, I'm never going to!'

* * * * * *

21

Lisa, Dave's pretty carer, Adrienne and Steve were in the staff room, since things were relatively quiet and the chance to have a break couldn't be passed by. Breaks were taken when the opportunity arose. You couldn't be sure about getting another one.

'You know, those huge Summer Fayre signs that go along the front of the home. Those blue and white boards with the date and time and things. Where are they?'

'Under the fire escape, Steve, aren't they?'

If you couldn't find anything, you asked Adrienne. The most thorough of cleaners, she knew every part of the home like the back of her hand.

'It's not that time of year already! Where are we going to put all the stuff? In room 10?'

'We'll have to sort out a date first, Lisa. That depends on the Manager and the owners. The Hindmarshes like to be consulted on these sorts of things.'

'Leave a note in the diary, Steve. We'll have to choose a date soon because we'll need to start collecting.'

'Mind you, we was lucky with the weather last year, remember? We had the only dry day the entire week! Let's hope we have the same again this year. Then some of the residents can sit outside. Perhaps we can raffle one of them!'

'If you can help me get those signs out some time, then Trevor can paint the new date on them.'

'Any time, Steve. Just let me know,' replied Adrienne.

Lisa was twenty-three and had been working at the home for fourteen months or so. Attractive and an avid party lover, she had an exhausting social life. This meant that she was not at her best first thing in the morning, especially a Saturday morning. This Saturday morning was no exception. Her head ached. Her thighs ached. She sipped her coffee. She'd asked to work this morning because she planned to be out again that evening. As far as Lisa was concerned, Saturday evenings were not made for staying in and watching television. She would be out with the boyfriend and her mates in some pub or other, or a nightclub, until the early hours.

The exception to this routine was when she was broke, which was once a month, just before payday. She would then be cadging cigarettes off anyone.

'Just one, thanks. You're a life saver!'

Yet, despite her erratic lifestyle, Lisa was a caring, conscientious and reliable young lady. The old people liked her. Perhaps they saw something of their own younger selves in her. The world in which Lisa lived was, maybe, not so very different in some ways from the world they remembered growing up in.

'I'll ask my mum for some Avon bits for the raffle. No harm in asking, is there?'

Over £400 had been raised at the previous year's Summer Fayre. This money was kept separate from other monies in a residents' bank account to which only Joan, Carol and Steve had access. Last year's money had been used to buy luxury items such as birthday presents for the residents. It also bought bubble bath and talc for those residents whose family didn't provide such items. The provision of toiletries was not included in the care home's fees. Neither was the hairdresser or the chiropodist.

The fund had allowed some of the residents to enjoy a day out at a local bird sanctuary in August. It had also been possible to take a few of them to a pantomime after Christmas. In recent years the local fire service had gained a glittering reputation for putting on a good panto. Organised in support of some charity or other, it was an evening of lunacy, mayhem and forced audience participation in the nearby community centre. Carefully-selected senior citizens from the home were able to forget their age and enjoy being young again.

Like all the residents, Ralph was accustomed to strangers being shown around the home, his home. Many were looking for a room for their aging relatives. As one of the consequences of his stroke, Ralph's speech was indistinct and he had difficulty in communicating effectively. However, being a determined man, he usually managed a few discernible words to indicate his genuine delight at seeing visitors. He was also able to make gestures. Appropriate gestures, thankfully. Ralph was always hoping that when the new resident arrived it would be another man with whom he could strike up a friendship. He accepted that it was difficult for anyone to have a proper conversation with him these days, but the thought of future companionship was one motivation for him to persevere with efforts to speak clearly.

The small group made its way along Ralph's corridor, led by the home's Manager, Mrs Jenkins. There was some snippet of conversation about a special diet, Ralph thought.

'Sweeteners, the cook will use sweeteners. We have several diabetic residents. Ah! This is Ralph. Good morning Ralph. How are you?'

Mrs Jenkins didn't wait for Ralph to attempt a reply. She gestured and the visitors followed her into Ralph's room.

'There, you see? Its not too difficult to make a room look homely.'

The visitors were predictably impressed.

'Your father can bring in bits of furniture. As long as it's not got woodworm or whatever. A favourite chair, a small bookcase, some army photos or some of the family, that sort of thing.'

Ralph's room was tastefully decorated with personal mementoes. Pictures and photos had been hung on all the walls. If a room was to be shown off to visitors, it was Ralph's. And Ralph kept his room tidy, which made him very popular with Adrienne.

Mrs Jenkins had much to do, but a high room occupancy level was vital for the good of everyone, so time had to be made for these tours. She had found that a tour could be completed in fifteen minutes, plus a five-minute chat in the office to bring things to a tidy conclusion. Upon returning to her office she handed the visitors a copy of the home's brochure.

'You'll find the home's contact details in this booklet. Don't hesitate to ring me if you have any questions. If I'm not here the staff will help you. I'm sure our staff will do everything to make… I look forward to hearing from you…Thank you for your interest… It's been a pleasure.'

The elderly Mr Sainsbury would now have to be persuaded by his three daughters to become a resident in a care home. Ralph had heard Mrs Jenkins remark that the man could bring army photos in with him.

'An old soldier' thought Ralph to himself. Once again, he was full of anticipation.

* * * * * *

It should come as no surprise to learn that there were those among the residents who did not know what time of year it was. Or what day of the week it was. Or who the current prime minister was. If you asked they would probably say Tony Blair. Their mental faculties had deteriorated to the point where they seemed to be living either in the distant past or in a continuous 'now', unable to remember the recent past and unable to anticipate the immediate future.

An assortment of daily newspapers was delivered to the home each morning, the delivery time depending on school terms and school holidays. The cost of the papers was met by the resident concerned. Thus it was that some of the residents at The Golden Farthing Care Home were very much aware of the world around them. Natural disasters such as floods in Asia or earthquakes in South America, political scandals, bombings, the contestants in X Factor or the runners and riders at Ascot, none of these things was able to pass by entirely unnoticed. For others, events seen on television or read about in the tabloids could have been taking place on another planet. The distinction between fiction and fact, between *Coronation Street* and *Panorama*, was blurred and no longer understood. These residents were perpetual spectators of events that never touched their lives.

Sometimes a resident's mental state deteriorated to the extent that even a wife or a son would no longer be recognised. This was a cause of considerable distress for those concerned. And so it was that Fathers' Day, Sunday June 21st, dawned to a very mixed reception.

For Ralph it would be a day for receiving genuine affection from his family back home. It would be a day spent with Vernon, his eldest son, with presents, gin and tonics, home cooking and good company. Ralph would come back to the home at about seven, tired out but happy in the knowledge that he was valued and appreciated.

Both Vernon and Patrick were in business, the elder in computer software for industrial robots and the younger in banking and finance. They both worked hard, earned enormous salaries and had expensive, palatial homes. They both managed to find some time for their father, even if it was just popping in for ten minutes on the way home from work. They took turns at having their father home for Sunday lunch, so every fortnight dear old Ralph would be at one or other of his son's homes being fed and watered, entertained by his grandchildren and feeling that his life had been productive and useful. Perhaps he was just another item in their overloaded diaries, but they both seemed to have a genuine commitment to him and rarely missed their turn at having him home.

No greater contrast could there be in Fathers' Day celebrations than that between those enjoyed by Ralph and those refused by Dave. Who could know what went on in Dave's head? He lived in his own world, at odds with everyone else. His son Paul would visit regularly, but was often unrecognised. Dave had only been out of the home three times since the day of his admission and two of those had been attempted escapes. The tale was told that on one visit from his son, Dave had gone down the corridor to the loo and refused to come out until staff could convince him that Paul had gone home. Nevertheless, there would be a visit sometime during this Fathers' Day from a very loyal son.

For Ted and Samuel, the only other male residents in the home, there would be visits from family members during the day and cards from distant and not-so-distant relations with expressions of remembrance, love and devotion. Each card would be put in the recipient's own room or placed in one of the lounges for a few days.

* * * * * *

The care home inspection team, known as Care Standards, arrived at nine thirty on Tuesday 23rd June. On this occasion the team was made up of two women and one man. Joan showed them to the office and then went to the kitchen to organise some coffee and biscuits. Steve was in charge, as Primrose Jenkins was enjoying a holiday in Spain.

Inspection visits were either 'announced' or 'unannounced'. The former, as in this case, were advertised by phone and letter a month in advance. Posters were supplied to inform residents and their families of the impending visit in case they wanted to raise some matter with the inspectors. These announced inspections took place at least once a year. On the other hand, any number of unannounced visits could be made, some of these out of hours at weekends or late at night.

The purpose of each inspection visit was to ensure that the premises and the level of care provided were of a satisfactory standard. There were umpteen pieces of legislation with which the home had to comply. There were Health and Safety laws, Food Safety laws, Fire

Safety laws, Employment laws. The staff had to be properly trained, the electrical equipment had to be properly tested and the residents had human rights.

The long list of statutory care home administration items had to be inspected and approved. Rachel Stevens and Kimberley Thimble would work their way through this paperwork as efficiently as possible. Though both women were Registered Nurses, neither had worked in a care home; having experience of care homes was not a pre-requisite for inspecting them. Fire alarm log books, resident registers, accident books, nursing care plans, complaint forms, staff criminal record checks and a thousand other matters would be duly scrutinised.

The third member of the team was a retired butcher, Gordon Knox. Gordon now made his way to the ground floor lounge to talk informally with some of the residents.

Because this was an announced inspection, written details of which the Manager had received a month prior to the visit, there had been more than enough time to ensure that everything appeared to be in order. For instance, in those weeks when the fire alarm test had been overlooked, an entry would nonetheless be entered into the fire log book. Resident care plans that had been dormant for months would be updated and rewritten to give the impression that they were frequently referred to and regularly revised. The many resident assessments would also be reviewed and updated. Nutritional assessments, wound assessments, Waterlow or Norton Scale assessments (for predicting and avoiding bed or pressure sores), incontinence assessments, mobility assessments, assessments for the use of cot-sides, assessments of inappropriate behaviour, assessments of the likelihood that a resident might wander off the premises - if it could be assessed, it was. There is nothing like an impending inspection to motivate staff in the creative updating of all these matters.

Similarly, the kitchen record books would confidently show that fridge and freezer temperatures were rigorously noted three times daily as required and were always satisfactory. The testing of food temperatures would appear to be done regularly and to be satisfactory. The mantra of the day was that if something had not been recorded, it hadn't been done, even if it had been. This attitude was seriously flawed. Someone's initials in the kitchen cleaning record book was not evidence that the fridge had been cleaned. A tick in the bath book was no guarantee that the resident had been bathed. If ticks and initials needed to be seen, then ticks and initials would be provided. The greater the mountain of paperwork, the less chance the records would tell the truth.

Rachel and Kimberley waded through the list, never questioning the validity of anything they were presented with or doubting any word that fell from Steve's lips.

'Let's move on to the kitchen then, shall we?' said Rachel. The women picked up their checklists and left the office to make a visual inspection of the kitchen, its microwave, toaster, cooker, fridges and freezers, its floor, walls and ceiling. They might decide to inspect the fridge and freezer temperature record book, the food temperature record book, the food thermometer calibration record, the kitchen cleaning record book and the food store, but these were often left to Environmental Health Officers to look at on their inspection visits.

Mr Knox had, in the meantime, wandered into the lounge.

'Hello, how are you?' he said to one of the residents. Dave gave him a blank look.

Don't give away any secrets, Dave. Don't put your life in danger. Keep quiet.

'I'm Gordon Knox. My friends and I are visiting the home today and checking to make sure that you're comfortable living here.'

Be strong, Dave. Be strong and brave. They want you to talk and give the game away. Don't let them make you, Dave. The escape, remember the escape. You'll never escape if you give the game away.

'Are you happy here? Have you made new friends?'

Dave looked away as if he hadn't heard. Mr Knox realised that he had chosen the wrong resident. He thanked the silent man and moved across the lounge.

Well done, Dave! Brave Dave. The plans for the escape are safe. No secrets given away. Good old Dave!

Dave had a broad grin on his face as he clapped his hands together loudly, got up and walked out of the lounge.

'Good morning, I'm with some friends who are visiting the home this morning. Checking to see that all is well. The name is Gordon.'

'Good morning to you, sir! I'm Ted White.'

Twenty minutes later, having had a couple of useful and illuminating conversations with residents and staff, Mr Knox joined his colleagues on their tour of the home. They were in the laundry. It would probably take all day to look at every room in the place, but every room would be looked at.

* * * * * *

Mrs Jill Hindmarsh was making her way to Salisbury. Her father had not been too well in recent weeks, so she was planning to spend a couple of days with her parents. She made frequent visits to see them, not least because she loved Salisbury for its shopping. On this occasion she was bringing some groceries with her and two new pairs of trousers. Though her elderly mother was still quite active, she didn't share her daughter's love of shopping. Jill would take it upon herself to go through her father's wardrobe and replace old trousers with new.

Later that day a dark metallic blue BMW with a new registration would drive into the Hindmarshes driveway.

It was past six-thirty when the inspectors finally left The Golden Star Care Home. All seemed to have gone well. Nothing dreadful had been discovered and no embarrassing mishap had occurred. A written report of the findings would be received by the Hindmarshes and by the Manager within a few weeks. It would also appear on the inspection team's website for anyone to read. Copies of these reports were always made available to members of the public.

QUIZ

Some suggested answers are in italics.

'The majority of the residents didn't have any say when it came to the when, where and by whom of bathing. They were simply told at what time and on what day they would be bathed. They would be bathed by whoever was available.'

13. If this was <u>your</u> care home, what would it tell visitors about the quality of care you were providing for your residents?

- *The quality of care is not like that expected in a care home, but more like that expected in an institution.*
- *Residents are not involved in decisions being made on their behalf.*
- *Residents are treated as if they were children, being told what to do.*
- *The quality of care is adequate, in that residents are bathed regularly and do not smell of urine or faeces. Incontinent residents are bathed more often to prevent their skin being excoriated.*

'Lisa was twenty-three and had been working at the home for fourteen months or so... Yet, despite her erratic lifestyle, Lisa was a caring, conscientious and reliable young lady. The old

people liked her. Perhaps they saw something of their own younger selves in her. The world in which Lisa lived was, maybe, not so very different in some ways from the world they remembered growing up in.'

14. What has Lisa's life got in common with the earlier lives of her residents?

- *Parents who might not understand young people.*
- *The need to get a job and earn money.*
- *Enjoying parties, dancing and nights out.*
- *Wanting a new boy/girlfriend.*
- *Dumping your boy/girlfriend.*
- *Planning to get married.*
- *Avoiding getting pregnant.*
- *Liking new clothes and wanting to be fashionable.*
- *Hearing about wars all around the world.*
- *Smoking!*

15. In what ways is Lisa's life easier, better and safer than the earlier lives of her residents?

- *Better healthcare.*
- *Immunisations against diseases.*
- *Contraception easily available.*
- *National Minimum Wage.*
- *Holidays abroad.*
- *Computers and the internet.*
- *Mobile phones.*
- *National Health Service.*
- *Health and safety laws at work.*
- *On line shopping.*

- *Childcare, nurseries and child minders.*
- *The right to maternity leave and maternity benefits.*
- *Nicotine patches!*

'Like all of the residents, Ralph was accustomed to strangers being shown around the home, his home.'

16. What is it about your care home that makes it feel homely for your residents?

- *Having personal items with you such as photographs, ornaments or a rocking chair.*
- *Matching fabrics such as curtains, carpet and bedspread.*
- *Meals that take into account your preferences.*
- *Likes: brown bread, blue cheese, red cabbage, black pudding.*
- *Dislikes: greens.*
- *There are no unpleasant smells.*
- *Feeling safe and secure.*
- *Being allowed to go outside, or wheeled outside for a cigarette.*
- *Having friends and family call and visit.*
- *Being spoken to by your own name.*
- *Having somewhere to lock away your valuables.*
- *Being allowed to drink alcohol.*

17. Does your care home feel like a home or an institution? What's the difference?

- *Your answer.*

My own opinion is that a care home is where the needs of an individual resident are put first whenever possible and practical. An institution is where the needs of individuals are largely ignored.

Rather than the routine being planned around individuals, in an institution the individuals have to fit in with what is organised.

'It should come as no surprise to learn that there were those amongst the home's residents who were unaware of what time of year it was. Or what day of the week it was.'

18. *Autumn's Colours* **highlights some of the ways in which dementia and confusion show themselves in the lives of our residents. List as many as you can find.**

- *Dave talking to himself, planning an escape and seeing everyone as an enemy.*
- *Residents unable to eat their food without getting into a mess.*
- *Residents using knives and forks upside down.*
- *Residents eating food with their fingers.*
- *Some residents not recognising family and friends.*
- *Residents not knowing what day of the week it is.*
- *Dave walking into the rooms of other residents at night.*
- *Vera wanting to get up and go shopping in the middle of the night.*
- *Residents unable to have a sensible conversation.*
- *Some residents not able to differentiate fact from fiction.*
- *Old Rose never wanting a window open, even in summer.*

'The greater the mountain of paperwork, the less 'accurate' it was likely to be.'

19. **It's a common complaint. Too much paperwork! List some of the paperwork that you think is unnecessary or a waste of time.**

- *Your answer.*

My opinion is that the assumption, 'If a task hasn't been recorded, it hasn't been done,' is fundamentally flawed. It's an unsafe assumption to think that a task has been completed simply because a tick or an initial suggests that it has. Care home managers, owners and inspectors should overhaul and review what paperwork is needed and what records are required to be kept, with a view to reducing it by fifty percent.

CHAPTER THREE

THE CARE HOME

You'll find the Madding Crowd Care Home in the picturesque and atmospheric town of Dorchester in West Dorset, Thomas Hardy's Casterbridge. From Dorchester it's an interesting drive along the A35 to the shopaholic's paradise known as Bournemouth, the destination of many a sun-seeking and beach-loving holidaymaker over the decades.

In the past Dorchester had the dubious distinction of being the town with the highest ratio of three-car families. To the north-east is the uniquely beautiful and sacred city of Salisbury, its cathedral towering above neighbouring buildings. And only eight miles to the south, a short and exciting journey over the Ridgeway, lies the intimate town of Weymouth. From the Ridgeway is signposted the aptly named 'Came Down Golf Course'. Resculptured in places for the 2012 Olympics, much of Weymouth looks the same as it did when King George the Third visited it some time ago.

In bygone times Dorchester was a much smaller and more rural town. Parts of it still look rustic and unchanged from previous centuries and the days when Judge Jefferies sent the Tolpuddle Martyrs to a warmer climate. But despite its fascinating history, the local authority felt the need to earmark strategic sites for housing, retail and industrial development. Consequently, new housing estates appeared, one of which was the Castle Park Estate with its accompanying array of supermarket, post office, school, themed pub and garage. This part of the town, changed beyond recognition, lies in the shadow of Maiden Castle, a 6000-year-year old earthwork that remains unchanged and sentry like, surviving as a vast and grassy monument to earlier human settlements.

After a series of planning applications and appeals, another housing estate was nearing completion. Spreading to the dual carriageway that separates the twenty first century from the remnants of a fourth century temple that our Roman friends built on Maiden Castle, was the Maiden's View Estate. It was here that the Hindmarshes had a detached house at the end of a cul de sac, far from the madding crowd.

* * * * * *

The Hindmarsh's care home was not a new, purpose-built structure. It was a converted building. Most visitors agreed that a reasonable job had been made of the conversion. Doorways were widened for wheelchair access, ramps with handrails replaced steps at the front and back of the building and three lounges were provided, one on each floor. Other rooms were turned into an office and a staff room, the latter, thankfully, some distance from the residents' areas. A spacious laundry was created and the old lift replaced with a new model. The kitchen and the main dining room had been placed next to one another, something that might seem obvious, but which is evidently not obvious to all architects.

In former days Dorchester had enjoyed its own small hospital, Dorset County Hospital in Princes Street, a solid-looking stone structure with blue metal fire escapes scarring the exterior. Other small hospital units were spread around the town. With the town's expanding population these facilities were initially enhanced by putting Portakabins on the Princes Street site as a temporary measure.

These had formed the Children's Unit and the Geriatric Unit, as it was then called. Eventually, to the relief of almost everyone, it was decided that money would be better spent building a completely new hospital for Dorchester and the surrounding villages on a new site away from the town centre, so the old hospital was closed and sold off to developers. One of the satellite units sold off at the same time was a geriatric unit in Damers Road. It was this unit that Mr and Mrs Hindmarsh purchased and converted into their 40-bed care home.

The Trumpeting Major Care Home for the Elderly and Infirm of Casterbridge therefore looked grand and elegant. Stone walls merged with double glazing. The main entrance was right of centre and led into a foyer. This has been designed to serve as a reception area with an administrative office, but it was found that there was no need for a receptionist, so it became a store for resident records and other documents, alongside zimmerframes.

Primrose Jenkins managed the day-to-day running of the home from her office down the corridor. A large photograph of Brian and Jill Hindmarsh was displayed ostentatiously in the foyer and a small spotlight in the ceiling highlighted the smiling couple.

On the whole, the Hindmarshes were reasonable proprietors and employers. Little was known about their background, since they sought to keep their personal lives well away from their business activities, but they appeared to be a normal middle-aged couple. They chose not to interfere with the running of the home, since neither of them had any nursing or medical experience. It was said, however, that they had once had a female relative in a nursing home who had died in tragic and mysterious circumstances. The passage of time and the absence of hard facts had allowed the details of this dark episode to be embellished. Was there any truth in the story that the old lady had been murdered by another resident?

When the Hindmarshes came into money from somewhere they

decided to buy their own care home. The rumour that they were big national lottery winners was doubted, but could not be altogether dismissed.

The couple generally visited the home at least once a month, usually by prior arrangement with Mrs Jenkins, staying for an hour and discussing matters of the moment. They would introduce themselves to any new residents and members of staff. Brian would also call in each Saturday morning to collect any residents' fees, sign cheques and, as he said, to make sure that all was well.

Alas, the home had little in the way of lawns or gardens. It could only boast a couple of very small flower beds and several concrete troughs. Some of these had daffodil bulbs planted in them, forgotten all year round until they made a welcome display each spring. The others had various bits and pieces growing in them, planted by an elderly bow-legged man who was employed to do the gardens.

In fact old Frank was not actually paid for his labours. His frail old wife had died at the home after a long illness some three years back. Having been a regular visitor during Beryl's slow demise, he had missed his visits when she eventually died. With time on his hands, he had volunteered to look after the flower beds, which had until then been woefully neglected. And so, from time to time old Frank would appear in his green apron and wellies to 'do the gardens'.

* * * * * *

Mealtimes were often hard work at The Mince and Mash Care Home for the Masticatorially Challenged. Breakfast was the easiest meal of the day, because it arrived in several stages. Folks had their porridge or Weetabix, their tea and toast. They seemed to want none of the alternatives. Perhaps there weren't any. But dinner time was different.

It's time for your rations, Dave. What do you have to do, Dave? I have to eat it all. I have to eat it all. All of it. You need your strength, Dave. Remember the escape. You'll need your strength. The situation is grave, Dave. Be brave, Dave!

'Dave, use your knife and fork!'

Wendy took a paper napkin from the nearby trolley and wiped Dave's gravy-covered fingers. She put the knife and fork in his hands.

'Now try to eat properly.'

Be brave, Dave.

* * * * * *

Dinner was served at one for most residents. The 'feeders', who couldn't manage to feed themselves and needed various levels of assistance, were served earlier. Twisted arthritic fingers might be a problem for some, while for others it was remembering what to do with a knife and fork. For both care and kitchen staff it was easier to cope with lunch by having two sittings. The other residents appreciated this, since sitting next to the likes of Peggy or Dave and watching them eat could be enough to destroy the heartiest of appetites.

The dining room was furnished with eight square tables, each accommodating four people. On each was a tablecloth of some description, four plastic place mats and a small vase of silk flowers. The tablecloths didn't match one another these days. The green chequered ones had been brought in by 'laundry Clare' who had bought them in a car boot sale.

And so Dave and Peggy sat at one table with Wendy attempting to stay in charge of proceedings while Eve was sitting at another with Tracey to help her. Tony had cooked chicken and mushroom pie, carrots, broccoli and potato, which he'd pureed for Eve.

'There you are, you lucky people! Get that down you!'

Wendy's task was to ensure that the equally muddled Peggy and Dave didn't try to eat each others' meals, which they constantly seemed to find more appetising than their own, that they didn't use their fingers to eat with and that the food went more or less straight from plate to mouth. Each wore a plastic apron to minimise collateral damage. Salt and pepper pots, vinegar bottle, sugar bowl and silk flowers were all put out of harm's way.

'If ever the expression 'second childhood' was applicable to old people, it's at mealtimes' said Wendy out loud.

She could remember the day when, not long after Peggy had moved into the home, her family had decided to take their mother home for the afternoon and return her after tea. This, they had announced with evident self congratulation, was going to be a regular thing. It turned out to be an isolated event and the experience was never repeated. What caused the change of mind was never disclosed, but it wasn't hard to guess.

It's an unfortunate fact of life that even the best food, when it has been pureed, seems to imitate other substances with disgusting accuracy and manages to look quite inedible. But, for Eve there was no viable alternative. Semi-solid food was difficult for her to swallow, so Tony would puree her meals. She was also encouraged to drink nutritionally-fortified drinks. Soup, yoghurt and pureed meals were regularly offered to her and though she would attempt to eat something, she didn't manage very much. Tracey patiently tried a few teaspoons of pie, then a couple of yoghurt, followed by a sip or two of tea from a spouted drinking cup. This took all of twenty minutes.

Eve was then returned to the secure familiarity of her room. She was suffering from a malignant growth somewhere in her bowel. This would eventually be the death of her, but in the meantime it caused her to tire easily and she needed a lie-down in the afternoon. With the aid of a hoist the ever-capable Tracey lifted the ever-delicate Eve on to the protected bed, covered her in a crocheted blanket, drew the curtains, raised the cot-sides, put her buzzer and a drink within reach and left her to enjoy some rest. Dave and Peggy walked back to the lounge with Wendy. The dining room could now be made ready for the remaining residents to enjoy the fruits of Tony's labours.

As was the case in the lounges, so it was in the dining room. There were no set places and residents were free to sit where they pleased, but most residents had their chosen or allotted place and woe betide anyone who dared to sit in it. Some of the most spiteful exchanges between residents occurred as a result of someone sitting in the wrong seat.

With thoughtfulness and imagination Tony had compiled three seven-day menus. He had put these into clear plastic A4 envelopes and pinned copies on the back of the kitchen door and stuck copies on the dining room wall. They were supposed to be followed in rotation. The residents had no say in the compiling of these menus. They ate what they were given. Cost was the governing factor, not resident's choice or preference.

Not that Tony's meals were poorly cooked or the portions meagre. They were nothing of the sort. They looked appetising and were nutritious. It would be doubtful if many of these residents could have eaten so well had they remained in their own home and lived from a state pension. Yet despite this, and the efforts Tony put into providing an adequate meal, each lunchtime saw a disheartening amount of waste.

'You would never think that this was the generation that experienced food shortages and had to get by with ration books' an offended Tony would complain as he scraped food into a black bucket.

* * * * * *

'Ah, Bev, just the person I'm looking for.'
'Oh no, I don't like the sound of that!'

'Busy?' asked Anna.

'Of course…! No, not really. What is it?'

'You're needed in room 18 until the next buzzer goes off.'

The relatively quiet hour between two and three was an opportunity to make some progress in the preparations for the Summer Fayre. All sorts of items were appearing in room 18, which was looking more chaotic as the days passed and the great event approached. Although an unoccupied double room, it looked far too small to store the growing mountain of carrier bags and boxes. Anna wasn't sure where she and Bev ought to begin.

'I'll tell you what. Shift everything up this end where the beds are, look, and as you sort it out put it down that end. Clothes by here and other things over there.'

'Right.'

Since Anna couldn't think of anything better, she settled for Bev's suggestion. Slowly, without much enthusiasm, books were sorted from knick-knacks, children's books from adults and clothes into men's and women's. Pictures were put into one large cardboard box and jigsaws into another. Pricing all of this would be a headache, but one that could wait until another day.

* * * * * *

At seven each evening Samuel would press his buzzer for the carers to hoist him into bed. This evening was no exception to the rule. Sometimes he would have to wait several minutes for staff to arrive, which he presumed was because they were busy attending to someone else. Sometimes it was. Sometimes it was because he had to wait for someone to come in from outside where they were having another fag break. Such was not the case this evening, however. He soon heard footsteps approaching his room and the door being knocked, a rare courtesy that Samuel appreciated. Tracey and Val entered.

'Evening Sam.'

'Evening Sam, my precious!'

Samuel couldn't see very well and had difficulty in distinguishing faces, but he recognised voices. Since moving into the home he had grown to prefer some carers above others. Tracey was one of his favourites. He felt safe with her.

'Hello my dears! Are you still here, Tracey?'

'I'm working a double shift today and then I'm off Friday and the weekend.'

'Lovely, my dear.'

'You ready to get into bed, then?'

Samuel was not a particularly big man, but even without his legs he was probably around the thirteen stone mark. A portable electric hoist that was kept on charge in the corridor was brought into the room. The two carers manoeuvred the red nylon sling behind his back and down around his thighs. The straps were clipped to the arms of the hoist and Val pressed the button.

'Hold on tight!'

Sam held on tight. He was lifted up until he was out of his wheelchair and dangling in mid-air. He was then pushed over his bed and lowered on to it. The straps were detached and Sam was rolled to his left and then to his right to release the sling.

'Lovely, my dears. Lovely. Thank you both very much.'

'You're welcome. Is that all, Sam?'

Tracey folded up the wheelchair and put it against the wall.

'Yes, that's all, my loves.'

'Goodnight Sam!'

'Goodnight!'

Sam's diabetes had been diagnosed soon after his retirement at sixty-five from the Post Office. He was now eighty. Since his diagnosis he had lost both his legs below the knee. The loss of the first had been an especially traumatic event and one that he had struggled to come to terms with. He had been so active, walking the streets as a postman and playing bowls in his leisure time. The recent amputation of his other leg was less of a trauma in that Samuel could see history repeating itself. He was also becoming partially blind in his left eye. The problem with his feet had been due to worsening blood circulation which had led to a blackening of his toes and to gangrene setting in. This was not an uncommon problem for diabetic sufferers, as was the worsening of his sight.

Samuel understood that his sight was only going to get worse and that the longer he lived the greater were the chances of his going completely blind. May had been unable to cope with her husband's second amputation, coupled with his increasing degree of blindness.

'I think it's for the best, really,' she would tell the neighbours, their friends from the Dorchester Bowling Club and her fellow worshippers at Bethel Baptist Church. 'I mean, he has all the attention he needs and they can keep an eye on him day and night. They do regular tests for his diabetes, so he's in safe hands.'

Despite knowing it was for the best, May found the nights very lonely after so many years of marriage. Their companionship, the core of every marriage, had been removed.

Samuel had read the ninety-first psalm many times in his large print Bible. He knew it by heart. He found the psalms to be a great source of strength.

'The best medicine of all!' The old man closed his eyes.

'He who dwells in the shelter of the Most High' he whispered.

He let the words sink in. Samuel had for many years dwelt in the shelter of the Most High. This evening's meditation was brought to a close with a prayer in which he thanked God for the care home and for carers like Tracey. He asked God to comfort May, now alone at home, and to bless Matthew in his work as a doctor in Kenya. He was hoping to see his son when he came home for a few weeks in the summer. He would probably see his wife the following day.

'Amen' whispered the old saint.

QUIZ

Suggested answers are in italics.

'Breakfast was the easiest meal of the day because it arrived in several stages. Folks had their porridge or Weetabix, their tea and toast. They seemed to want none of the alternatives. Perhaps there weren't any.'

20. What was the probable reason why the residents didn't want any of the alternatives?

- *There really were no alternatives.*
- *There were alternatives, but the residents weren't told about them.*

Wendy took a paper napkin from the nearby trolley and wiped Dave's gravy covered fingers. She put the knife and fork in his hands. 'Try to eat properly.'

21. Who might Dave be talking to, or who might be talking to Dave, telling him to be brave?

- *The person is entirely imaginary.*
- *The person is someone who Dave knows.*
- *The voice is someone Dave used to know, but who's been dead for years. His mother, for instance.*
- *Dave thinks it's God talking to him, or the devil, or his guardian angel.*

22. Does Dave ever take any notice of what the voice tells him?

Yes, he seems to.

- *He has twice managed to escape from the home.*

- *He refused to speak to Gordon Knox, a member of the inspection team that visited the home.*

23. Why is Dave using his fingers to eat his dinner?

- *He's not concentrating on what he's doing.*
- *He's forgotten how to use a knife and fork.*
- *He wants to be annoying!*

'If ever the expression 'second childhood' was applicable to elderly people it's at mealtimes' said Wendy out loud.'

24. What might have prompted Wendy to make this remark to herself? *Both Peggy and Dave were performing like badly behaved children.*

'You would never think,' an offended Tony would complain as he scraped food into a black bucket, 'that this was the generation that experienced food shortages and which had to get by with ration books.'

25. What could be the reason for this disheartening amount of waste?

- *The meals were unattractively presented.*
- *The meals were not cooked properly.*
- *The portions were too big for small appetites.*
- *The staff took so long to serve the meals that they were cold.*
- *The residents were allowed to eat too many snacks between meals.*

'Tracey was one of Sam's favourites. He felt safe with her.'

26. What would be your attitude to Samuel if you were <u>not</u> one of his favourite carers?

• *Your own answer.*

27. What could <u>you</u> do to become one of his favourite carers?

• *Take time to know and understand him.*
• *Remember his individual ways, his likes and dislikes.*
• *Because of his poor sight, always identify yourself so that he knows who is caring for him: 'Sam, it's Chris. I'm putting clean underwear away in your drawers!'*
• *Remember that he is poorly sighted, so describe things to him.*
• *'Your cup of tea is on the left of the table.'*
• *'Here's your dinner, Sam. Sprouts are at two o'clock and chicken at seven o'clock.'*
• *'What TV channel do you want?' 'The controls are by here.'*
• *Ask what colour clothes he wants to wear. 'Is it the blue shirt or the red, today, Sam?'*
• *Offer to read a passage from the Bible to him.*
• *Show some interest in his family. Ask after his wife or his son.*

28. As a carer, is it wrong for you to have favourites among your residents?

• *Your answer.*

My opinion is that we all have favourites in all areas of life. Friends, work colleagues, neighbours, etc. No, favourites are fine as long as you don't make it obvious. You should treat all your residents with respect and not treat some better than others. Treating one better than another would be discriminatory.

'Despite knowing it was for the best, May found the nights very lonely after so many years of marriage. Their companionship, the core of every marriage, had been removed.'

29. Suggest three single words that might accurately describe Sam and May's many years of marriage.

• *Devotion, long-suffering, happy, fulfilling, loving, close, committed, strong, dedicated, loyal.*

30. What are (or will be) the four most important aspects of <u>your</u> marriage.

• *Your own answer.*

My opinion is that companionship will be a central aspect of it!

31. What will be the effect upon your marriage (upon you and your partner) when <u>your</u> partner becomes a resident in <u>your</u> local care home?

• *Torment.*
• *Relief.*
• *No more sex.*
• *Sexual freedom.*
• *Loneliness.*
• *New relationships.*
• *A strain upon the marriage.*
• *The end of the marriage.*
• *Suicidal.*
• *Ecstatic.*

CHAPTER FOUR

ROSE'S SECRET

Ralph had been living in The Golden Horizon Home for Aged Gentlefolk for almost five years. His room was on the first floor and this morning he was sitting in the rocking chair which had been an imaginative and much appreciated birthday present. The *Daily Mail* on his lap was open at the television page as he pressed the green button on the remote control. It was approaching eleven and the cricket coverage would soon be starting. He used to play the game when he was younger and understood that cricket was a game of tactics.

The footsteps in the corridor were, Ralph assumed, his mid-morning mildly warm coffee being brought to him. But the footsteps didn't reach his room. They were followed by more footsteps and the voices of strangers. A door opened.

'There's something going on in room 14, it sounds like.'

He pressed the 'mute' button. Ralph was sure he could hear a couple of women's voices and a man's. The door remained ajar for a few minutes, then opened and closed. Voices faded down the corridor. Geoff Boycott was standing in the middle of the pitch, microphone in hand, speculating silently about England's chances of bowling the Australians out. The footsteps and voices returned. This time the door opened, the voices went in and the door was closed.

Today was to be the day Toby Sainsbury gave up his independence and became a resident in a care home.

Convincing eighty-two year old Toby that he should move into a care home had been easier than Andrea had anticipated. He had lived for many years in Queens Avenue, a most attractive area of Dorchester made up of spacious and individual-looking houses with mature trees and wide pavements. His three daughters, all married with children, lived around the town. Barbara had died many years ago and Toby had coped very well until recent events. A burglary shortly after Christmas had made him a nervous man. He was unhurt by the intruders who smashed the glass in the back door to get in. He had been asleep on the settee at the time and the noise had woken him. Perhaps the burglars had assumed that the house was unoccupied, until Toby began shouting. His voice scared the intruders off, but not before they had taken money from the kitchen table.

Some weeks after the break-in, Toby had fallen in the bathroom. A laceration on his head had needed some stitches at the Accident and Emergency Department. The fall had shaken him, and he realised that he had been lucky not to break any bones. Dr Taylor had visited him at Andrea's request to give him a general check-up and had found his blood pressure to be higher than it should be. He hadn't been able to say with any certainty what had caused the fall. It could have been a bit of dizziness due to the blood pressure problems, or just an unfortunate slip.

'While I'm here, though, it might be a good idea to take some blood for routine testing' said the doctor.

So, just in case there was something amiss, Dr Taylor had taken blood and urine samples for a general analysis.

Following this fall, Toby's daughters had taken turns to call on their father each morning to check he was out of bed and had eaten some breakfast. They would call again in the evening to wash up and tidy the living room. This had worked for a while, but they soon found themselves exhausted. Joanne had a young family which took up much of her time. Andrea and Vicky had teenagers who took up even more time. They would have to think of something else.

The blood and urine samples had revealed a mild degree of diabetes, known these days as type 2 diabetes. The surgery nurse had called on Toby to take further blood samples and these had confirmed the diagnosis. The outcome was that Toby would have to take a diabetic tablet each morning and restrict the amount of sugary food he ate. He started to find sugar-free items appearing in his larder following Andrea's shopping trips. He had never heard of Canderel before. It was following one such shopping trip that his daughter summoned up her courage.

'Dad - Jo, Vicky and me have been thinking that the time has come for you to think about making plans to move into a care home.'

She thought it best to leave the matter there and allow her father to digest her suggestion. She would return to the subject later in the week. The suggestion had taken the old man by surprise, and he'd been hurt by the directness with which his daughter had spoken. On reflection, though, he knew there was a good deal of sense in what Andrea had said. The house was too large for him. He had hardly been into the garden since the previous autumn. He knew he needed someone to keep an eye on him, to do his laundry and his shopping. His age and health were causing concerns. He was adamant that he didn't want to become a burden to Andrea, Vicky or Joanne.

The sisters called on their father on the days following the suggestion about the care home, though the subject was never mentioned. They concentrated on the bits of shopping he needed, the washing and ironing of his clothes, the paying of the milkman and the newsagent and the collecting of his pension. But at the end of the week Andrea returned to the subject.

'Have you had any thoughts about moving into a care home, Dad?'

He had.

A trembling skeletal left hand reached from a blue armchair towards a framed photograph perched upon a chest of drawers, Lucy's own chest of drawers that she had brought into the home with her. The hand seemed to be finding the frame too heavy to pick up. It dragged the frame slowly towards the old lady until it lost its grip and the picture fell into her lap.

'My dear Doug' said Lucy softly. 'My dear Doug. If you could only see me now. I wonder what you would say to me, my dear Doug. What would you say?'

Lucy stared at the photo. For several long moments she stared at it. Once again she sought to bring the man's portrait up to her face. Inch by inch, trembling all the while, Doug came closer to her. She kissed him and the trembling photo slowly sank back into her lap.

*　*　*　*　*　*

'My dear girl, must it be now?'

'Yes, Mrs Jenkins, if you don't mind.'

Mrs Primrose Jenkins and Miss Zoe Mitchell sat on either side of the office desk. One sat in a dark red leather upholstered chair, the other on a grey plastic chair. The one was secure and certain about her future, the other was feeling insecure and uncertain about hers.

'Now, what is it that's so important?'

'I think I might be pregnant.'

'You only think you are?'

'Well, I'm late with my period and when I done a test it was positive.'

She shrugged her shoulders.

'And I just know I'm pregnant.'

'Well, if you girls will play with…'

She didn't finish the sentence, and there was a long pause while

Mrs Jenkins put some papers in an envelope. Zoe was nervous. She wondered if she was supposed to say something else. Eventually, Primrose Jenkins, married with no children, asked Zoe a question.

'I don't know at the moment. I'll have to let you know.'

'You'll have to put this in writing, my dear. And you must let me know the expected date of delivery.'

'I will, as soon as I know.'

'Very well. Is that all?'

'Yes, I think so. Thank you.'

Zoe closed the office door behind her and made for the back door, her cigarettes and lighter in hand.

* * * * * *

'Anna, Lucy looks upset. Do you think you could have a look at her? I asked her if she was feeling unwell, but she said it was nothing. But she isn't right, I don't think.'

'OK, I'll go up in a minute, Dot.'

Dot was already disappearing back to the laundry. Lucy was about eighty. She was a shrunken and shrivelled old woman who weighed about five stone and whose skin seemed barely to cover her bones. A stroke had completely paralysed her down her right side. She was a frail scrap of a thing who took a lot of looking after, but she seemed to endear herself to people. She seemed to be the sort of person someone went into care work to look after. Anna went upstairs and along the corridor.

'Hi Ralph!' she called as she passed.

She arrived at Lucy's room and went straight in. Lucy was still sat with the photo in her lap. The truth was that she hadn't the strength to put it back on the dressing table.

In a sudden flash of remembrance, Anna recalled having a conversation with someone about Lucy some time ago. Apparently the same upset had occurred at what must have been the same time last year. Was that a year ago, already? There was a folded-up wheelchair behind the door, and Anna unfolded it and sat in it, manoeuvring it to be close to Lucy.

'Is it the anniversary, Luce?'

Lucy nodded.

'Is it the anniversary today?'

Lucy nodded. Anna held the old lady's hand in hers, very gently. It was cold. She picked up the photo.

'Was he a good man, Lucy?'

'He was a good man,' Lucy replied softly, putting an emphasis on the word 'good'. 'He was a good man to everybody.'

Several of the staff could remember meeting Douglas Anderson, though not Anna. He had been Lucy's second husband. What had become of the first, Lucy would take to the grave with her. She never mentioned him. Lucy and Doug had been happily married for many years. Her stroke had occurred about four years ago and was the reason for her admission to the home. She had been severely disabled by it, losing the use of her right arm and leg, with the result that Doug had been unable to cope with her needs at home.

The two of them had never been apart for any length of time before and this enforced separation caused both of them considerable grief. In effect, it ended their marital relationship. They were no longer husband and wife, as most of us understand the expression, but patient and visitor. And Doug had been a regular visitor to his beloved Lucy. Three times each week he would arrive, on the bus or by taxi. Christine would bring her father in each Friday afternoon, because she finished work at lunchtime on Fridays.

Lucy had been unprepared for her husband's sudden death exactly three years ago, the sixth of August. Apparently he had collapsed and died in the garden.

'He loved his garden, did my Doug.'

His death had seriously affected his wife, who wept and wouldn't eat properly for many days afterwards. She was desperate to attend his funeral, but Colin, her son by her first marriage, had decided she was too frail to cope with such an event. She had been made to feel abandoned and was to this day very sad and bitter towards her son. She had lost all enthusiasm for life. 'I've been robbed of any need to live' she would whisper.

So she sat in her blue plastic covered armchair, her catheter bag half full beside her and the photo of Doug in her lap.

'Yes, he was a very good man.'

'Today's Thursday' thought Anna. 'Christine will be in tomorrow. Best to leave Lucy on her own with her treasured memories. No need to contact the family.'

Colin lived somewhere in the Midlands, as far as Anna knew. He might have visited Lucy at some point, but such a visit would have been a rarity. He had fallen out with his mother a long time ago, probably over her marriage to Doug. Neither of them seemed willing to repair the breach in their relationship. Colin had not even visited his mother when Doug had died, to the very vocal disgust of some of the staff. He had communicated the funeral arrangements to Christine, having her tell Lucy that they would not be taking her to her husband's funeral. Christine also resented Colin for his treatment of the old lady. Anna sat with her precious little Lucy for several minutes. She put her arm around the old lady and kissed her on the forehead.

'I'm sure he was a very good man' she said.

* * * * * *

The front door bell rang. As Amy reached the foyer she could see

Evangeline Jacobs, 'Darset born and Darset bred', standing at the door with three carrier bags in one hand and a large box under the other arm. The double lock was slipped back and Evangeline made her entry.

'Thank you, Amy.'

'You're welcome. You look loaded! Are they heavy? Do you want me to carry something? Shall I carry one of the bags?'

'Bless you, child! Aye, take a couple of they bags. That's right!'

The two of them set off down the corridor.

'Are these things for your mum's room, then?'

'Oh no, my lover, these aren't for our Winifred. They's for the summer show. I promised Primrose a couple of my paintings for the raffle. And in that box there's some jams from last autumn. You may as well 'ave some of they, too. They keeps well enough.'

They stood outside the manager's office and Evangeline took the bags from Amy and put them on the floor. She knocked on the door, and without waiting for a reply went straight in.

'Weird woman!' said Amy to herself.

In fact Evangeline was an industrious and talented woman who earned her living by painting other people's pets, from prize-winning bulls and rosette-adorned pedigree dogs to scruffy family pets. And she made wines, pickles and jams.

*　*　*　*　*　*

The preparations for the home's Summer Fayre were gathering pace. Room 18, barren of any occupants, had been set aside for storing clothing, books, china, still more clothing and what could only be described as junk. Items were sorted and priced as time allowed. Several black bin-bags of clothing judged to be 'beyond' were disposed of by Trevor, the handyman. Adrienne had pulled the two huge hardboard signs from under the fire escape stairs and dusted them. Trevor had then tied them to the railings along the front of the home, having updated the date from last year. So now the whole neighbourhood could make plans to support The Golden Treasures Care Home Summer Fayre.

* * * * * *

Dave glanced up from the catalogue he was looking at. A smart-looking man dressed in a suit and a bow tie had knocked on the door of his room and was walking in.

'Hello!' the smartly-dressed man was saying. He was putting a briefcase down on the floor. Now he had picked up a chair and was sitting almost opposite him. Dave thought it best to say nothing. He didn't trust these people. He knew that he recognised the visitor, but he couldn't remember who he was.

'Hello, Dad. Are you talking to me today?' said the stranger.

* * * * * *

Old Rose's well-kept secret came to light in a most unexpected way. Nobody at The Happy Memories Home for Weary Pilgrims was remotely aware of any aspect of her early life. This was the case with many of the residents. Staff only caught a glimpse of their childhood, adolescence or early adult years if they chose to talk about their past or if relatives or friends mentioned something. As might be imagined, some were only too happy to tell of the hardships of their younger days, of living through the war, of ration books, of the time when they had had to make their own entertainment.

With Old Rose, little was known about her past, since she hardly ever spoke about it. She didn't speak much about anything. She was a plump old lady. Very plump and very old. She suffered considerable discomfort from a worsening arthritis in her arms and legs. She sat all day in front of the TV that was always on in the lower lounge. She was quite anonymous. She was got up in the mornings, toileted during the day and put to bed in the evenings. In between these activities she refused to eat her meals properly, preferring to eat numerous snacks brought in for her by friends from the nearby Bethel Baptist church.

Apparently Rose had never married, so there were no children or grandchildren. In fact there appeared to be no family at all. On arriving at the home she gave as her next of kin one of the Baptist Church elders. He would, she insisted, take care of all her affairs when her end came.

Anna was taken aback one morning when Old Rose made a request.

'If it's not going to cause too much trouble, since today is my bath day, I would like the girl Zoe to bath me.'

Sure enough, when Anna checked, it was Rose's bath day. But the old lady was not known for relishing the prospect of a bath. Moving from armchair to wheelchair and from wheelchair to bath hoist made her worn-out bones creak and was clearly painful. On the other hand, Rose did say that once in the water the warmth eased the discomfort a little. So a puzzled Zoe wheeled Old Rose into the bathroom, the bath already half full. The young carer carefully and painstakingly undressed the old lady, helped her shuffle on to the bath hoist, swung her around and lowered her into the warm water. She washed her all over and let her soak in the warmth for a few minutes. During all of this they exchanged some polite words and then Zoe hoisted Rose out of the water. Suspended on the hoist in mid-air, she was delicately dried and powdered and the top half of her dressed. She was then lowered to the floor and Zoe completed the drying and dressing.

All of this exertion made Rose breathless. She spoke in short sentences, catching her breath in the hot and talcum powdered air of the bathroom.

'Now, my dear,' said Rose, 'Are you young Zoe?'

'Yes, I'm Zoe,' replied Zoe.

'Well, my dear, I've something important to say to you, some advice as you might say.'

'Have you? What's that?'

'Look, sit down for a moment, my dear.'

Zoe was about to pick up a hairbrush, but on hearing the tone of Rose's voice she put it down and sat on the chair.

'Now, I've something to tell you, my dear, that's for your ears only. Do you promise me that you'll not tell another soul?'

The old lady stared at Zoe, who nodded.

'I understand that you are...' she hesitated, 'with child, my dear. Is this so?'

Another nod. Old Rose continued in short, breathless sentences.

'I was once in the same predicament as you, my dear. With child and without a husband. But, as sure as I sit here I have never seen that child, my child, from the day I gave birth to him to this very day.' She paused for breath again.

'I was in service, my dear, to a very well-to-do, well-off family' she continued. 'I was about your age, Zoe my dear, about sixteen, and I lived in the attic of the family's mansion house. In a room set aside for servants. Well, the master of the house, the lord of the manor so to speak, a man about the age of my own father, had his way with me, if I may put it like that, on one occasion. Only the one occasion, mind you. I don't want you to think I was a loose young woman, my dear. I'm convinced that he behaved as he did because he believed me to be young and naïve, which I was of course.

'Well, when he discovered I was expecting his child he had me sent away to serve in another large house far away for me to have the baby there. Can you believe that? But the worst part was that after I had given birth the baby was taken away from me. Snatched away! Just like that! As if it didn't belong to me! It was a boy. Whether he was taken to an orphanage or adopted by someone, I don't know to this very day.'

Zoe leaned over and tore off some toilet tissue. She handed it to Rose, who wiped tears from her eyes.

'Of course, you have to understand that I was so young in those days, added to which a servant girl didn't have much say about anything.'

'No.'

Old Rose leaned forward and placed a bent and arthritic hand on Zoe's knee, as if to emphasize the gravity of what she was about to say.

'Now, my dear, what I most wanted to say to you, the point of me telling you this, is this. You make sure that you look after that baby of yours when it arrives. The best gift you can give to your infant is to be a good and caring mother, a loving mother. A devoted mother. Being a mother was something that was denied to me. Sad, but there it is. Promise me that you'll do all you can to be a good mother to that baby of yours.'

'I promise!'

'And mind you don't tell a soul what I've just told you.'

'Oh, no. No, I won't tell anyone. Not a soul!' whispered a gob-smacked Zoe.

QUIZ

Suggested answers are in italics.

'Convincing eighty-two year old Toby that he should move into a care home had been easier than Andrea had anticipated.'

32. Toby is worried about moving into your care home. What could he be worried about?

- *Is he going to be properly looked after?*
- *Will he regret the decision?*
- *Are his family going to visit him regularly or slowly forget about him?*
- *What will become of his house, his furniture, his gardening tools?*
- *Will he make new friends?*
- *What will become of his savings?*
- *Will he be able to make phone calls?*
- *Will he be allowed to go out with his daughters for the day?*

33. What benefits will Toby enjoy when he moves into your care home?

- *No worries for him or his daughters about shopping, cooking his meals, washing up.*
- *No worries about washing and ironing his clothes.*
- *No worries about heating bills.*
- *His medicines are ordered for him and given to him regularly.*
- *He can make arrangements to visit his daughters or they can visit him whenever it's convenient.*
- *He has constant supervision and care.*
- *Should he have another fall, help is at hand straight away.*

'Mrs Primrose Jenkins and Miss Zoe Mitchell sat on either side of the office desk. The one was secure and certain about her future,

the other was feeling insecure and uncertain about her future...'
'Now, what is it that's so important?' 'I think I might be pregnant.'

34. **If you had been listening to this conversation what thoughts might have been going through your mind?**

- *Mrs Jenkins disapproves of Zoe getting pregnant.*
- *Mrs Jenkins is jealous of Zoe being pregnant because she has no children.*
- *Zoe is being made to feel ashamed of what she has done.*
- *They represent two generations who do not understand or appreciate one other.*

35. **Which of the following might be a carer in your care home and which a resident? And which could be either? How do you decide?**

Gemma	Edna	Zoe	Donna
Jade	Mabel	Beryl	Leanne
Gladys	Doreen	Winifred	Anne
Victoria	Emma	Ruby	Daisy

You probably decide by thinking of people you know with these names. I have <u>never</u> cared for a resident called Gemma or one called Donna! Who names their daughter 'Edna' these days?

36. **In what ways might Zoe Mitchell's future differ from Primrose Jenkins's future?**

- *Mrs Jenkins has a future which appears to be predictable, Zoe's future is not.*
- *Mrs Jenkins has a future that appears to be financially secure, Zoe's future is not.*
- *One is in a stable relationship, the other not. Ah, but which one? Don't pre-judge people!*

'Lucy had been unprepared for her husband's sudden death, exactly three years ago to the day, the sixth of August. Apparently, he had collapsed and died in the garden.'

37. Lucy and Doug were unprepared for something that was inevitable. How could this have been avoided?

- *Nobody is able to predict the time of their death, but as age creeps along it would be wise to think about the fact that you will be on your own one day, or that your partner will be.*
- *By discussing aspects of death with your partner.*
- *By making a will.*
- *By making family members aware of funeral matters such as burial or cremation, favourite hymns.*
- *By making sure insurance policies are able to be found easily.*
- *By making sure that organ donor wishes are known about.*

'Rose's well kept secret came to light in a most unexpected way.'

38. Why do you suppose Old Rose kept this matter a secret for so long?

- *Because she was ashamed of it.*
- *Her attitude was, 'It's none of your business!'*
- *It was in the distant past and didn't matter to Rose any more.*
- *She thought she might be criticised for not trying to find the missing child.*
- *She thought somebody else might try to find the missing child.*

39. What might be the reason for Rose telling Zoe about it?

- *She believed they were both in a similar situation, though generations apart:*

- *A man had 'had his way' with each of them.*
- *Each was 'with child' as a result.*
- *Each was pregnant without a husband.*
- *She wanted Zoe to be a good mother, to value motherhood.*
- *She was still grieving for her lost child.*
- *She felt the need to tell someone about this incident before she died. Elderly people often feel a need to tell someone about something that is not generally known before they die.*

40. If you were Zoe would you promise Rose that you would tell nobody about her secret?

- *Yes, and I wouldn't tell anyone.*
- *Yes, but then I would tell the manager or her deputy and stress that what Rose told me was in confidence.*
- *The story, at face value, should be officially noted in Rose's resident file. Though very unlikely, there may be legal problems regarding 'next of kin' when Rose dies. Best to make a note of Rose's story and be prepared for the unexpected.*

CHAPTER FIVE

DECORATION, DEATH AND THE DAY OF THE FAYRE

'At least my home's got some colour in it, if you know what I mean. Our bedroom's pink and grey. Walls, curtains, bedspread, all coordinated like. All matching, if you know what I mean. Then in the kitchen we've got green and yellow, cheerful colours. Well, we spend so much time in the kitchen because we have our main meals in there.'

Wendy was sitting with Steve and Dot in the staff room, their morning break nearing its end.

'The latest is that my youngest says he wants his bedroom done in Manchester United' she continued, 'Walls, lampshade, curtains, duvet, you name it.'

Wendy had one son left at home. The others had moved out and the second eldest was still in prison. Mark, the Manchester United fan, seemed to be given everything he wanted. His mother had once boasted that she had spent over £400 on him one Christmas.

'The duvet set is twenty-five quid for a start. The curtains is another eighteen. That's in the Argos catalogue and that's as cheap as anywhere.'

What had triggered off this conversation was the fact that each bedroom was usually redecorated between one resident leaving it and another moving in. Room 10 had been empty for a few weeks, and this morning was evidently the morning Trevor was going to paint it. From the staff room window he could be seen unloading his decorating tools and tins of paint from the boot of his car.

Some would say that the term 'redecorate' was a misleading one when applied to Trevor's appointed task. Room 10 wouldn't look much different when he had done the job from the way it looked now. It might look a bit cleaner, but there would be no change of colour. There would be no colour. There was a distinct lack of colour throughout the Pastel Rainbow Care Home. There was no Daffodil Yellow, Candy Pink, Warm Apricot or Eggshell Blue. Only Monotonous Magnolia. That one colour was dominant throughout the entire home. Lounges, dining rooms, corridors, office, toilets and all forty bedrooms were almost entirely magnolia.

On the brighter side, there were paintings and photos hung on most of the walls. Outside the office hung an impressive view of the care home as seen from the air, a photo taken from a passing satellite.

The reason given for this insipid colour scheme was the projected cost of constantly having to redecorate the home in a dozen different colours. Trade quantities of magnolia could be purchased at a fraction of the cost of smaller quantities of other colours. Steve politely listened with half an ear to Wendy's monologue. He found the Hindmarsh's attitude to redecorating the home unconvincing. Any saving on paint was such a small sum seen in the context of the home's overall running costs. A vivid colour here and there would make such a positive contribution to the residents' environment. As Wendy pointed out, a home has colour in it.

Wendy was a good talker when she got going. Not having a husband at home for much of the time, she missed adult conversation, and made up for this by taking every opportunity to talk at work. Steve listened, trying to show some genuine interest in the various avenues of Wendy's life. He had worked at other care homes where the same approach regarding decoration had prevailed. There was Ivy Lodge, a home not far away built on three floors consisting of fifty bedrooms, three lounges and various utility rooms. And almost entirely magnolia throughout.

*　*　*　*　*　*

Steve took his breaks later in the morning because of the ten o'clock drug round, which he endeavoured to start at nine and have completed by eleven. It was the biggest of the 24 hours and could be finished by eleven if there were not too many interruptions. But there were relatives with questions both sensible and stupid, doctors, dentists and chiropodists calling, social workers phoning, sales reps appearing from nowhere to extol the virtues of some wonderfully-engineered appliance or newly-developed substance, delivery men wanting to know where they could put whatever it was, telephone engineers to sort out why the payphone wasn't working and staff saying, 'Sorry Steve, I know you're very busy...'

His coffee break over, Steve went into room 3 to have another look at Eve Parkes and give her a small drink, either of water or some fruit juice the family had brought in. But one look at the body in the bed told him there was no need. At last, Eve had passed away.

Familiar as he was with the deaths of residents, Steve still had to stop and think about what he should do first. He walked over to Eve and placed two fingers on her neck. There was no pulse. The pupils were dilated. Her chest was still. He looked at the clock. He pulled the bed sheet over Eve's head, closed the bedroom door behind him and went to look for a carer. He found Tracey in the upper lounge, collecting cups.

'Tracey!'

He beckoned her out of the lounge. He didn't want to broadcast the news just yet. Other residents who might be interested would be told of Eve's death later in the day.

'Eve's passed away. Can we wash her and so forth in a minute, before we start toileting for lunch?'

'Yes, if you want to.'

'Are you busy?'

'No, not particularly.'

'Can you get some wipes, a flannel and a towel? I'll meet you down there.'

Back in the office, Steve rang Eve's doctor. The woman he spoke to assured him that one of the doctors in the group would call over lunchtime to certify death. Then he rang Eve's daughter, Stephanie, to inform her of the sad news and to express his sympathy. Stephanie would make arrangements with the funeral people for family and friends to see Eve for the last time and pay their respects at the Chapel of Rest, rather than at the care home.

Steve collected a couple of plastic aprons and some latex gloves and returned to room 3. Eve's death had been expected, thanks to the cancer in her bowel. This growth had blocked her gut some time around last Christmas and she had had to be admitted to Weymouth Hospital. An operation to remove the growth was out of the question. Eve was too old, her general health too poor and the spread of the cancer too extensive. Some sort of colostomy had been performed to bypass the obstruction and thereby relieve some of the symptoms. It was a means of buying some more time, some more life. At ninety and in her debilitated condition, she was fortunate to have survived such an ordeal.

There had been a slow deterioration ever since. Eve had grown weaker and thinner. She sometimes appeared to have a yellow tinge to her skin, which suggested that secondary growths, metastases, were forming in her liver. Her appetite became progressively poorer and in the end it was as much as the staff could do to persuade her to drink a few sips. Those who had been nursing for some time knew that Eve's days on Earth were drawing to a close. When room 3 became vacant she had been moved from her upstairs room to this one, because it was near to the office and allowed constant supervision of its occupant.

Steve wrote 'No Entry' on a piece of paper and taped it to the door. Then he entered the room and put on an apron and gloves. He moved the bedside cabinet and pulled the bed away from the wall so that he could get around that side of the bed. Eve's body was still warm. She had not been dead long before Steve found her.

He had written the time on the back of his hand. It was one of the details he needed to complete the Notification of Death Form that would be sent off to the local authority. Gone were the days when 'Last Offices' involved packing all body orifices with cotton wool to prevent body fluids escaping. Things were simpler these days. Eve Parkes would be washed all over, a fresh colostomy bag placed over her stoma in case of leakage and her dentures put into her mouth if they still fitted. A clean nightdress would be put on, her hair would be brushed and all jewellery removed with the possible exception, depending on the family, of a wedding ring. This would be taped over and the fact noted. A clean incontinence pad would be put in place and then Eve would be left alone, awaiting collection by the undertaker.

Jewellery would be taken to the office, signed for by the two of them and then locked in the safe until collected by Stephanie. The curtains were left closed and the room tidied. The family had agreed that Eve would be buried next to her husband.

Following the doctor's visit, Steve would ring the undertaker and Tom Sykes would call early in the afternoon and remove the body to the Chapel of Rest. He would clearly remember burying Arthur Parkes.

Small wafer like discs about the size of a ten pence piece were handed to Samuel and Harriet.

'After supper he took the cup…' recited the Reverend Paul Lane.

Very small clear plastic cups, each holding about a teaspoon of communion wine, were then offered and taken by Samuel and Harriet.

'As often as you eat this bread and drink this cup…' the vicar continued as the wine was drunk.

There was no praying, just the reading of a prayer or two from the Order of Service book. There were no devotional words of comfort drawn out from any Bible verses. There was no restating of fundamental Christian truths. The Reverend Paul Lane had been asked to 'do communion' for the residents, and this he thought he was doing. An opportunity to be of real spiritual benefit to two elderly saints of God was either being overlooked or ignored.

Like many care homes, the Advancing Horizon Home for Aged Pilgrims had asked a local minister to call once a month to provide holy communion to those residents who wished to receive it.

'Some of our residents have spiritual needs, Vicar,' Primrose Jenkins had informed the Reverend Lane, 'and since we are in your parish it seems in order to request that you or one of your colleagues attend to those needs.'

The Reverend Lane had assured Mrs Jenkins that he would undertake to call each month to offer communion to her residents.

'If for some reason I can't make it, I'll ask one of my deacons to stand in for me. I'm also the chaplain for Dorchester Prison. And of course the hospital keeps me quite busy. I'll do my best, however.'

Mrs Jenkins pondered how much more desperately the convicts needed the vicar's help than did her residents. Never mind. Though not a particularly religious person herself, she was aware that some of her residents might be. And the fact that a local minister provided Holy Communion each month was something else to be included in the home's brochure under the heading 'Other Benefits Provided Include...'

'The present generation may not be a churchgoing one, but previous generations attended church or chapel regularly' she said. 'Though I doubt very much if morals were any higher then.'

* * * * * *

The day of the Silver Birches Care Home annual Summer Fayre finally arrived. The prayers for good weather had been answered. The day had started off dull and cloudy, but was now bright and cheerful. Two o'clock approached and there was a healthy queue forming in the car park. The home was truly a hive of activity. Only rarely could the place be described thus.

The kitchen, normally a place of some orderliness was particularly fraught, because two cooks were sharing the kitchen. Michelle was there to cook lunch for the residents, while Tony concentrated on producing items for the Fayre. His skills came to the fore as he prepared imaginative creations for the cake stall. Tempting pastries filled with fresh cream and dipped in plain chocolate, fresh strawberry tarts, sponge cakes and iced fairy cakes were all neatly placed upon china plates with doilies. It was a certainty that the cake stall would be sold out well before the end of the afternoon.

Since Tony had such skills, one would have thought he might be somewhat frustrated and not a little wasted working in a care home. Imaginative flair and creative artistry were not often called upon. But he was happy enough in his work.

Folding tables from somewhere had been delivered on the back of a truck and placed all around the edge of the car park. On three of these tables clothing of all kinds was heaped, with Joan in charge of it and under strict orders to get rid of as much as she could. On other tables there were neat rows of books and piles of magazines, adults' at one end and children's at the other. Readers Digests were in a box on the ground. Other tables had all manner of china bits and pieces. The items that had looked such a jumbled mess a few weeks ago were now sorted, priced and out on view to the town's bargain hunters.

The tombola had been left to Adrienne, who sat behind her table with Ralph assisting her. Most of the staff were involved with the Fayre in one way or the other and some of the residents had been press-ganged into helping, too. Enough staff remained on duty to ensure that residents were not neglected in the general excitement of the afternoon and that Dave didn't manage to escape and run off down the street again.

Lunch had been served promptly at one and then the tables cleared and the dining room given 'a good going over' in preparation for the sale of refreshments. Hot and cold drinks, hot dogs with or without onion and burgers with or without relish would be available. The tables had matching paper cloths. The CD player on the windowsill which normally repeated the hits of Frank Sinatra was given the opportunity to play something more up to date. Music brought in by Lisa was described by Nancy as 'very bright and cheerful'. 'It's hip hop, Nance!'

As two o'clock came and went, the throng invaded the premises and the pushing and shoving began in earnest. Bargains were searched for and claimed. By teatime the residents fund would be another £400 to the good.

*   *   *   *   *   *

It was one of those nights when Dave couldn't sleep. His room was directly above the ground floor lounge and he could be heard moving about. Periodically he could be heard walking down the corridor to the toilet, and more importantly walking back again. In these restless moods he was likely to wander into someone else's room or to try to escape again. Past experiences had taught the night staff that there was really no alternative but to bring him downstairs. So Debbie sat him facing the television with a blanket over his legs.

'He seems settled enough.'

'Put his feet up on a stool, Deb. And a pillow behind his head. He might drop off. You never know your luck.'

Debbie did as Pauline suggested. Dave showed no signs of being tired, but there was always the hope that he would drift off, eventually. A mug of tea and a handful of biscuits were beside him.

'Sometimes his night sedation works and sometimes it don't.'

'Perhaps he needs a stronger tablet.'

'He's already on twenty milligrams. And other meds during the day. It's a wonder he can keep his eyes open!'

'Anyway, we've got plenty of channels to choose from. Have a look and see what's on the film channels. Anything exciting?'

'Let's have a look. Where's the TV pages?'

'On Old Rose's chair, look.'

Pauline scanned the film channels for something that fitted the mood.

'What do you fancy watching, girls?'

'What's the choice? I couldn't believe this when I came in the other night. I wonder what persuaded the Hindmarshes to get satellite TV put in for the residents.'

'Put in for the night staff, you mean!'

QUIZ

Suggested answers are in italics.

'There was a distinct lack of colour throughout the Pastel Rainbow Care Home. There was no Daffodil Yellow, Candy Pink, Warm Apricot or Eggshell Blue. Only Monotonous Magnolia.'

41. How would having tasteful and imaginative colour schemes in your care home affect the lives of both residents and staff?

- *It would help the place feel like home.*
- *It could help poorly sighted or confused residents know where they were in the building if the floors had different colour schemes: 'I must be on the top floor because the carpet's blue.'*
- *The residents will feel valued if they are asked about what colours they want in their bedroom or lounge. Would I like someone to decide what my bedroom should look like? No! They might choose bright green or dark purple and I might not be too keen on either in my bedroom!*
- *The dining room would look more like a restaurant.*
- *Staff might feel that they were working in a home and not in an institution.*

42. What three single words might describe a care home that is Magnolia throughout?

Boring, cheap, institutional, uncaring, practical, unimaginative, miserly, economic.

'Eve's passed away.'

43. What will you do to support a resident who is dying, and the family of such a resident?

- *Continue to provide a good standard of care while he/she is alive.*
- *Take care that I don't avoid the resident or their family.*
- *Remember to talk about all sorts of things. Life goes on!*
- *Be prepared to talk about death with the resident if they wish me to, or -*
- *Refer this matter to a more senior member of staff to deal with.*
- *As always, be honest in my answers to questions. I shouldn't lie. If I'm unable to answer a question, I should say so and then find someone who can.*
- *I should be prepared to involve other people, such as a Vicar, Rabbi or Imam.*

44. Why should your residents die in your care home rather than in a local hospital?

- *They will receive a higher standard of care in my home.*
- *Our staff can take time to 'tie up loose ends':*
- *A family feud may need to be settled.*
- *A son or daughter living abroad may want to visit and say goodbye.*
- *The resident may want to see their solicitor to check or change their will.*
- *Hospital staff might see the dying person as a failure.*
- *Our resident can die more comfortably in familiar surroundings with familiar faces.*

45. When is the best time to talk about funeral arrangements with your residents and their families?

- *When the resident first come into the home. Such a general enquiry might seem normal and is often expected and anticipated.*
- *When the resident is taken seriously ill and death is a distinct and real possibility.*
- *Try to pick a suitable time. Be sensitive, but be 'up front' and 'matter of*

fact'. It is likely that the resident or their family may want to talk to you about such matters anyway, but are unsure about how to go about it.

46. All care homes have deaths. You should aim at 'good deaths'. What is a good death?

- *A pain-free death, where physical discomforts have been minimised.*
- *A worry-free death, where anxieties have been removed as much as possible.*
- *A death with family members present, if this is what the resident wishes.*
- *A death where all loose ends have been tied up.*
- *A death where the resident is aware that someone is with them. Dying alone should be avoided if possible.*

47. The family of a dying resident tells you that they want their relative to remain in your care home and not to be admitted into hospital under any circumstances. What do you do about this matter and what should the home do?

- *Remember that you are caring for the resident and not their family. You and the home must do what is best for the resident.*
- *However, the views of the family are important and should be treated with respect.*
- *You must tell the person in charge of your shift, immediately. Make a note in the resident's notes if this is the procedure in your home.*
- *This request can be agreed to without asking the resident, if the resident concerned is unable to express an opinion because they are too confused, sedated or in a coma.*
- *A terminally-ill resident should be better off dying in your care home than in a hospital.*

'The Rev Paul Lane had been asked to 'do communion' for the residents and this he thought he was doing.'

48. What contact might your residents have had with the Church over the years?

- *They were probably married in a church.*
- *They may have had their children christened in a church.*
- *They may have attended weddings and funerals of family and friends.*
- *They may have attended a Sunday school as a child.*
- *They may have had help and comfort from a chaplain when serving in the armed forces.*
- *They may have sung in a church choir as children or as an adult.*

49. In what ways might your residents find the visit of a vicar or priest to be positive and helpful?

- *It may help to maintain a link with friends who are unable to visit the home.*
- *It may help to reinforce long-held beliefs and strengthen faith.*
- *It provides opportunities to discuss personal problems and concerns.*
- *It provides an opportunity to report any abusive behaviour from staff or fellow residents.*
- *It provides a chance to talk about death, dying, heaven, hell, etc.*

CHAPTER SIX

SEPTEMBER SONG

This was the third time Maureen Biddlecombe had accepted Ray's invitation to have tea at his home. A strong relationship had developed between the two of them since Ray had been collecting her for the dysphasia clinic appointments. These clinic sessions were coming to an end, because Maureen's speaking ability had improved. She still slurred her words at times, but this slight impediment did nothing to interfere with or lessen the affection she and Ray felt for each other. They continued to find each other's company warm and stimulating.

Ray had been away for a week during August, on holiday somewhere in Spain with his son, daughter-in-law and teenage children. He was a much-travelled man and no stranger to Spain, but like most travellers he was always glad to get home. For him this was his beloved bungalow, neatly set in the beautifully floral village of Godmanstone, a few miles outside Dorchester.

On Maureen's first visit the two of them had enjoyed a drink and a bit of lunch in the village's famous Smith's Arms before returning to the bungalow, where they had sat together on a bench placed against the back wall and exchanged anecdotes about past times. They had both lived eventful lives and found each other's company relaxing and interesting.

On this third visit they held hands as they slowly walked around the colourful garden. Roses, marigolds, foxgloves, gladioli and many other plants and shrubs all made their natural contribution to fostering the growing romance.

'The garden's so beautifully kept, Ray! Do you really do all this on your own?'

'Yes, I do, though it's not too difficult because I make time to work on it regularly. It's a real labour of love. Any season, any weather, it doesn't matter. I can always be doing something useful out here.'

'Before I moved into the home I lived in a fourth floor flat, a comfortable flat with beautiful panoramic views and marvellous sunrises, but it only had a small balcony' she said. 'There's not much you can do with such a small space, so high up and so exposed to the wind and rain. I had a couple of containers with plants in them and that was enough for me.'

'Plants are good friends, Maureen. They just need to be understood and given some love and attention and then they'll give of their best!'

They moved on, stopping now and then to look at something of particular interest, the flowers, butterflies, birds and berries. Departing swallows sat on the telephone wires.

'It's surprisingly warm for late September, don't you think?' said Ray. 'No hint of an early frost and autumn's colours in the trees are quite stunning.'

'They're an amazing sight, Ray. In fact the whole village looks picturesque. It must be so inspiring in the spring.'

'At its best! Colours everywhere. Crocus, daffodils and all sorts.'

'Ray,' began Maureen, 'What would you say if I were to ask you to...' she faltered for a second. 'If I was to ask if you would like to look after me so that I could give of my best for you?'

She was immediately embarrassed by what she had said. In fact, she couldn't believe that she'd said it. Out of the abundance of the heart the mouth speaks.

Ray looked a bit puzzled. The question had caught him completely by surprise and he wasn't at all sure how he should answer it.

'Are you asking to be my wife, asking me if I would like to marry you, Maureen?'

She stood in front of him, put an arm on his shoulder and smiled at him.

'Yes, I am!'

'Well!'

'Ray, you're such good company. I really would love to live here with you. Truly! I'm sure you would do your best to make me happy and I'm certain I would do the same for you.'

'I know you would. I know you would.'

They walked a little further.

'You've taken me a bit by surprise. You'll have to let me think about this for a day or two. I'm not wishing to appear rude, and I'm not saying 'no' or 'yes'. You're worthy of a proper answer and I need a little time to think it over.'

'Of course you do. I understand. And you're not appearing rude.'

* * * * * *

This time it was Adrienne who answered the front door bell. She found a bespectacled woman who was surely well into her seventies if not more, dressed in a grey coat and matching hat with a brown shopping bag and a walking stick in one hand and a piece of paper in the other.

'Good morning,' said Adrienne very softly. 'I'm afraid all our rooms are full!'

'What?'

Adrienne spoke louder.

'Good morning!'

'Hello. I'm from St Saviour's Church. The one in Hardy Avenue. Do you know it?'

'No, I don't live in Dorchester.'

'Never mind. We have our harvest festival service next Sunday evening, not this Sunday evening, the one after and we wondered if any of the old folk would like to attend.' The lady handed the printed leaflet to Adrienne.

'The details are all on the leaflet.'

Adrienne glanced at it.

'The church will be decorated with all sorts of harvest produce, of course. Bread, vegetables, fruit and flowers and tins. It should look a lovely sight. I don't know if you've been to a harvest service, but its not a long service, if you take my meaning. It shouldn't be too long for those of your old people who have unfortunate personal problems. You understand what I mean? But the church will look so nice.'

'Well, maybe some of the residents will want to go along. I'll give these details to the Manager and if there are some who want to go, she can ring this number.'

'Yes, I see. Thank you very much.

'You're welcome!'

* * * * * *

Of all the visitors to the Silver Curl Care Home, one of the most popular was Veronica Page, a mobile hairdresser who spent every Monday fortnight at the home. She was well known because she had for many years worked in a hairdresser's shop in Dorchester called the Dorchester Hair Salon. In the spring she had quit working in the shop for reasons she never spoke of and had gone mobile, calling her business Clippings. From what she said it seemed that she had all sorts of customers from all over the place, and plenty of them. But Mondays

were quiet days, for some inexplicable reason, so she made that her
nursing home day.

Veronica was popular because she was so effervescent. Loud and
chatty, she was ready to talk to any of the residents about anything.
She never appeared to be put off by odd behaviour or confused
conversations, and her prices were reasonable.

'These are my special prices for the old folks, mind!'

There was a large white board in the lower lounge where
forthcoming events were supposed to be written before they happened.
The hairdresser's expected visit would be written on it, if the staff
could remember which Monday they were at.

'Is this Monday Veronica's Monday? Did she come last week?
Gladys, did the hairdresser come last week?'

'No, I don't think she come last week. Did she? I'm not sure. I
want to see her first when she arrives, mind.'

'I'll send her in to see you, Glad.'

Veronica set up shop on the first floor and used the nearby
bathroom. It was large, with a couple of basins that had mirrors behind
them. Most of the washing, cutting, colouring and perming was done
in this bathroom, but because the nearest electrical sockets were out
in the corridor the two dryers on their adjustable stands had to be set
up out there. By mid-morning damp towels and discarded hair were
everywhere. And from almost any point on the first floor Veronica's
voice could be heard. There was no doubt about it, her visits did the
residents a lot of good.

* * * * * *

Jade meandered up to the front door mat and gathered up the
assorted envelopes. The postman had arrived as usual, just before
lunchtime. He would push the mail through the letterbox and then

ring the bell to tell staff that he had been. Most of the mail would be addressed to the Manager or the Hindmarshes. Items for the residents were left on the office desk and passed on to them when someone was 'going their way'.

Jade began to sort them as she meandered even more slowly back down the corridor. Those for Mrs Jenkins or the owners she left in the office. Those for the residents she decided to deliver. There were several white envelopes for Enid, evidence that the family had not forgotten her birthday. There was another hospital appointment for George and a postcard for Olive.

* * * * * *

'Steve! What's Zoe doing?'

'She's upstairs, tidying the linen cupboard, Mrs Jenkins. I thought it looked like it could do with a sorting out. Do you want her?'

'I've a little job for her. Nothing strenuous. When she's finished, can you send her along to my office?'

Steve carefully trimmed the other half of Ted's moustache. He sat back to admire his handiwork.

'Looks fine, Ted!'

'How much do I owe you?'

Steve put his face up to Ted's ear and whispered. 'Nothing, Ted. But remember me at Christmas!'

He put the rinsed scissors and comb away in the bathroom cupboard. 'Well, she should have made an impression on the linen cupboard by now' he said to himself. He made his way up the stairs.

'How's it going, Zoe?'

'Getting there, slowly.'

'Primrose wants you. She said she's got a little job for you. She didn't say what it was, but she did say it wasn't strenuous.'

'I hope she don't want me to go round cutting fingernails. Bleeding fingernails!'

When the pregnant Zoe knocked on the office door and was bidden to enter, she learned that it was not fingernails. She was being given the task of asking the residents if they would like to attend the harvest service at St Saviour's. Arrangements would be made for the church to pick up residents and accompanying staff in a minibus. Zoe left the office and disappeared to the staff room for something urgent. Being wiser than in former days, she wouldn't ask all the residents. Twenty minutes later she was back in the office with her list.

'I haven't asked all the residents. I thought that would be asking for trouble. But of those I did ask, five said they would like to go. Five of the more sensible ones. Their names are on this list. I didn't ask Dave, but would he be allowed to go?'

'My dear child' whispered Primrose Jenkins.

Thinking her task had been completed, Zoe turned to the door.

'Wait a minute, I haven't finished.' Mrs Jenkins was looking at the staff rota.

'Today's Friday. Now then, Sunday evening. Who's on the late shift? Ah! You are. You and Joan. Would you feel up to going out with the residents?'

'Oh yes, I think so.'

'That will leave Clare, Wendy and Margaret on their own, but they'll be all right for an hour or so. My number's in the card file if there's a problem.'

Zoe went back to the linen cupboard, relieved that the fingernails would be someone else's task.

* * * * * *

'That was a missed opportunity, Dave, my boy. A missed opportunity.

A golden opportunity missed, my boy! A golden opportunity. You could have escaped. Escaped to freedom. I could have escaped. Yes. I could have run away from the church and escaped! A golden opportunity has been missed. A golden opportunity, Dave. A rare opportunity, Dave. She never asked me if I wanted to go. She never asked me. I wasn't given a chance. There'll be other opportunities, Dave. There'll be other opportunities. I wasn't given a chance. I wasn't asked. I'll wait for another opportunity.'

* * * * * *

Enid was in her room, opening her cards with a little help from Jade. Though her sight was poor, she held each card up to her face and commented on how nice it was, how wonderful and how thoughtful. As she looked inside each one, Jade read out the greeting and who the card was from. One had been sent 'from all at number six', but Enid insisted that she didn't know anyone at any number six. The cards were arranged on the chest of drawers.

'There's nice to have so many cards, Enid. How old are you today?'

'I think I'm about eighty, aren't I?'

'We'll all sing happy birthday to you at tea time. Tony's baked a cake for you and we'll sing happy birthday to you. Will you like that?'

'Oh, I expect so!'

'Will you manage to blow the candles out?'

'Oh, I'm not sure about that!'

* * * * * *

'How about Abbotsbury?'

'Abbotsbury, Joan? Not the Swannery again! Who wants to go and see a few swans, for goodness sake?'

An outing was being planned for later in the week. According to the weatherman, the warm start to the week was going to continue until the weekend.

'No, not the swans this time. Gee, that was awful, wasn't it? That was one of the worst days of my life. No, there's a farm sort of place near there with animals you can feed and pets you can pick up and cuddle. Have you heard of it?'

'No, I haven't. Have you heard of it, Jan?'

'That's right! The children went there for their outing with the school. It's mostly on the flat with plenty of animals to see. Cows and horses, sheep and what not. And you can buy packets of animal food to feed the animals with. I think this lot would love it!'

A small coach was booked with the Community Transport people and at eleven o'clock on the chosen day thirteen residents and five staff set out for the farm-sort-of-place. Wheelchair users had their chairs clamped to the floor in the specially adapted minibus.

Trish was the trained nurse who had drawn the short straw. In a cardboard box under her seat she had the midday medications, plus travel sickness tablets and an airway in case Daphne had one of her fits. Lisa had been given responsibility for the incontinence box, packed with pads, knickers, skin cream and plastic bags and gloves. Joan had charge of the packed lunches Tony had thrown together. These consisted of cling-filmed packs of sandwiches, flasks of soup, fruit scones and yoghurts. The coach was past the halfway point when Lisa announced to everyone that she had forgotten to put any pants in her box for the men.

'If any of you men has an accident,' she threatened, 'you'll have to make do with a pair of ladies' knickers until we get home!'

The choice of destination proved to be spot on. Access to everything was easy and residents were able to approach, touch and feed the animals. The cattle, sheep and goats were in sheds, while the ducks and hens wandered about freely. Numerous photos were taken of the residents with rabbits on their laps, foals eating from their hands and Dave holding a lamb that was only a few days old. At a later date these snaps would be put into a large frame and found a place on the lounge walls. It would provide a record of a most enjoyable day.

QUIZ

Suggested answers are in italics.

'…but this slight impediment did nothing to interfere with or lessen the affection she and Ray felt for each other.'

50. If Mrs Jenkins had been aware of the developing relationship between Ray and Maureen, what might have been her feelings about it?

- *Approving*
- *Disapproving.*
- *Surprised*
- *Condemning*
- *Supportive*
- *Delighted*
- *Awkward*
- *Shocked*

51. How do you feel about it?

- *Your own answer.*

My opinion? They're old enough to make their own decisions! Remember that loneliness in old age can, for some people, be very hard to cope with.

'We have our harvest festival service next Sunday evening... There was no doubt about it, Veronica's visits did the residents much good... The postman had arrived as usual, just before lunchtime.'

52. How are your residents going to keep in touch with their family, the local community and with the world at large?

- *By having access to newspapers, magazines, internet, television and radio.*
- *By letters and cards to and from family and friends. Staff may have to help with the writing of these, and provide stamps.*
- *By going out, with a member of staff if needed, on trips to the bookmaker, hairdresser, shops, pub, optician, pantomime.*
- *By having the community come to them. Hairdresser, vicar, school children, mobile library, dentist.*
- *By a resident's family paying to have a phone put into their room or by buying them a mobile phone.*

'Bleeding fingernails!'

53. Be honest - what aspects of caring for old people are (or would be) your least favourite?

- *Your own answer.*
I have a mega problem with green coloured sputum! Ugh!

'Enid was in her room, opening her cards with a little help from Jade.'

54. What makes this a happy little scene?

- *Enid is receiving uninterrupted personal attention from a carer.*
- *Jade is allowing Enid to open her own cards, rather than do it for her.*
- *Enid is given time to read and respond to each card.*

- *Jade gives help as and when it's needed.*
- *Jade reminds Enid that her birthday is going to be celebrated with other residents later in the day, with a cake that has candles and the singing of 'happy birthday'.*

'...and at eleven on the chosen day thirteen residents and five staff set out for the farm-sort-of-place.'

55. What benefits might Trish, the nurse in charge, Dave, a confused man, and Edna, who is not confused, get from this outing?

- *Trish -*
- *- A variation from the routine of the home.*
- *- A chance to enjoy a day out.*
- *- A opportunity to see the residents in a different context, to see them as real people and not only as residents.*
- *Dave/Edna -*
- *- A chance to vary a monotonous routine.*
- *- An opportunity to experience something different.*
- *- An opportunity to recall past experiences. They might have had pets in the past.*
- *- For Dave, an experience that might help him to live in the real world.*

56. When you're planning a day out for your residents, what factors do you have to keep in mind?

- *The residents' wishes.*
- *Obtaining the permission of the residents' families, if this is thought necessary.*
- *The weather forecast.*
- *Meals, medications, changes of clothes.*
- *That the transport is suitable for wheelchair users.*
- *Sufficient staff to cope with everything.*

- *Spending money for the residents and staff.*
- *Check insurance cover for the staff.*
- *Take first aid items and a mobile phone.*
- *Check that the destination is suitable for your residents. Does it have wheelchair access, ramps instead of steps, shelter if it rains, toilets for the disabled, and so on.*

CHAPTER SEVEN

PRESENT SENSUALITY
AND PAST SUFFERING

The night staff received requests for all sorts of things - painkillers, indigestion medicine, tea and toast, brandy, and help to dress in order to catch a bus and do some shopping.

'Vera. It's the middle of the night. There are no buses in the middle of the night. Now, please get back into bed.'

'My daughter will be waiting for me.'

'Not in the middle of the night she won't!'

Old Rose could be relied upon to buzz for her soluble paracetamols. She suffered so greatly from the grinding pain of her arthritis that she needed constant pain relief. These aches and pains didn't lessen at night and on a bad night the old lady would sleep in her armchair.

The main drug rounds took place mid-morning and tea time. A few medications had to be given in the early morning, but thankfully the custom of waking residents up at six with a cup of tea to swallow numerous tablets was on the way out.

Ted insisted on having his tablets early in the morning. An early riser for most of his working life, he still got up, washed and began dressing at about six. When he was brought his tablets and a half mug of tea he was usually at some stage of dressing. He disliked anyone interfering with his routine, so the tablets and tea were left on his bedside table for him to take in his own time.

Henry was a sufferer from Parkinson's disease, a degenerative disease that affected his ability to do almost everything. His movements were slow and his hands had a rhythmic tremor, but he eventually finished washing and dressing, although it could take up to an hour or so to complete. Although the disease was incurable, the symptoms could be controlled to a considerable degree by taking his Parkinson's drugs, four doses spread over 24 hours. It was important to take the first dose early in the morning, as soon as he got up, because within a half hour or so his shaking would lessen and his dexterity improve.

Water tablets were the reason for Ralph being woken at six each morning. He'd been diagnosed with heart failure, his heart not pumping blood around his body as efficiently as it should. There was a slowing down of his blood circulation, which allowed minute amounts of fluid to escape from his blood vessels into his skin tissues. Since water runs downhill, his feet would swell during the day. The water tablet made Ralph pass larger amounts of urine than usual for a few hours, reducing the amount of fluid in circulation and lessening the swelling. He would often have visitors during the day or be taken out in the car by one of his daughters-in-law. Giving him the drug so early in the morning would ensure its effects were over by the time any visitors arrived. Ralph, like many stroke victims, also took an aspirin tablet each morning, since it was believed to help in the prevention of blood clots.

Anna, the Deputy Manager, was endeavouring to update herself with the ever-changing prescription drug scene, part of her preparation for applying for a post in the local Intensive Care Unit. During the drug rounds she found it helpful to explain in simple terms to appropriate residents something about their tablets. This was something that the residents appreciated, too.

* * * * * *

Eleven o'clock on a Monday morning was the chosen time to test the fire alarms, if the requirement was remembered. If it was, an alarm would be set off from a different 'Break Glass' fire point each time. From the key cabinet in the office a black plastic gadget that looked like a match stick with a hook at one end was taken and poked into a slot on the underside of the chosen alarm. The alarm having been triggered and sounding off at a painful level, a quick but thorough tour of the home was made to check that all the alarms were ringing, all the emergency lights were on and all the automatic fire doors had closed. Staff then gathered at the designated fire assembly point in the entrance foyer.

The alarms were very loud and staff had to shout to make themselves heard, but fire regulations required that the alarms registered a specified level of decibels. What a valuable and combustible resident such as Beryl would actually hear as she slumbered each night under the influence of twenty milligrams of 'Perma-sleep' while the home burned down around her would depend upon whether she was in the habit of sleeping with her hearing aid in or not. However, it was necessary to warn everyone that the fire alarms were going to be tested, not least because it was important that new residents and new staff recognised the alarm when it sounded.

'Irene, my love, the fire alarms are going to be tested, don't panic!'
'What?'
'The fire alarms. They're going to be tested. Don't worry, it's only a test.'
'No? My arms? But I never wear a vest.'
'Irene, listen to me...'

* * * * * *

Tony was in work by seven each weekday morning and off at three each afternoon. Michelle was the part-time weekend cook, a quiet, middle-aged woman and a contrast to the talkative and outgoing Tony. On this particular Monday Tony stayed on after hours. He did this unofficially whenever he was baking and decorating a wedding or anniversary cake, and if the cake was at the delicate icing stage he was likely to stay until late in the evening.

Speciality cakes had been a sideline of Tony's ever since his appointment at the home. He was an excellent baker and his skilful decorating of cakes was almost unbelievable. Work would begin on a cake many weeks before it was required. Most would have alcohol in them, which meant the kitchen would smell like a pub the next day. Some cakes would be square, some round and some in the shape of a number. He used the home's facilities because his own kitchen had one problem, he said.

'Well, not to put too fine a point on it, it's the wife!'

He would leave his precious cakes wrapped in foil to mature for weeks in the kitchen storeroom, issuing gruesome threats in case anyone even thought to touch one of them. These cakes were not cheap. A three-tier wedding cake decorated with brightly coloured and ornate sugar scrolls, flowers and greeting would cost well into three figures. Taking many hours to complete, they were truly works of art. The charges reflected the time and uncommon skill put into the finished product.

* * * * * *

Ray had left the bedroom door ajar, so Maureen could hear him setting cups and saucers on a tray as he waited for the kettle to boil. She lay in the bed with her eyes closed, thinking how wonderful it had been to once more have a man she loved inside her. To her delight, the excitement had been surprisingly intense after so long. As she waited for Ray to return with the tea, Maureen Biddlecombe felt very content with life.

* * * * * *

The doorbell rang. Steve found Brian Hindmarsh waiting to be let in.

'Hello Brian!'

'Hello there, Steve. Sorry to have to ring the bell, but I came out without the key. How are things?'

'No problems, Brian. All's well. I take it you've called for the fees?'

'You've got it in one, as they say.'

The safe was installed in a corner of the office, and as they made their way down the corridor Steve noticed that Brian walked with a distinct awkwardness. They retrieved the resident fees and staff meal payments from the locked cash box in the safe. The amounts were counted and put into plastic envelopes and both men signed the cashbook. Brian was feeling some considerable pain in his left knee. He hoped nobody would notice, but was sure that everyone would.

'Well, it's been a lovely day for November, hasn't it? It's been a change to get out and do something in the garden. I'm afraid it's made the old joints a bit stiff, though. Probably trying to do too much all at once, I expect.'

'Aye, it's been a nice couple of days. Let's hope it keeps fine for our fireworks on Thursday. Will you and Jill be popping along?'

Brian hesitated.

'Yes, maybe. We might if Jill's back by then. She's been away for a few days at her parents. She likes to pop over now and then because they're not in the best of health. What time does it start?'

'About seven.'

'Ok, I'll mention it to Jill when she gets back, but I make no promises. If there's nothing else, Steve, I'll be on my way. I'll see myself out, thanks. Bye for now.'

He left Steve in the office and began walking with less inhibition down the corridor, pausing to look at the bird's eye view photo of the home on the way. Getting into the car was awkward. He wasn't sure if he had sounded convincing about working in the garden. Of course, he hadn't been anywhere near the garden all day.

'Oh well. She's worth it!'

Brian stopped the car at the exit for a moment, changed the CD and drove off. Moments later, a green Audi drove up to the front door. Ray got out and walked around the car, opened the passenger door, assisted his passenger out of her seat and escorted her up to the home's front door.

* * * * * *

It had been an uphill struggle trying to interest anyone in a fireworks display. Few residents seemed to be bothered about remembering the fifth of November and the gunpowder plot, so it had been decided to invite relatives and friends, staff members and their families to enjoy a buffet and firework display.

At the front of the home was space for seven cars, beyond which a low wall separated the car park from the pavement and road. The car park, emptied of its cars, was the only viable space for fireworks to be let off with relative safety. The residents' fund had purchased a selection of appropriate fireworks from a local store and this had been supplemented by a gift from the butcher from whom Tony ordered his meat each week. Although Andrew was not as cheap as the supermarket or wholesaler might be, Tony found that he was able to 'ask for a little favour' on such occasions as these.

'Think of it as an unofficial loyalty card sort of thing. I'm a loyal customer and Andrew looks after his good payers. Everyone's happy!'

And so burgers and sausages could be served, with jacket potatoes and vegetable soup. The evening was dry, but it was cold and the hot food was appreciated. Several parents stood stoically with their children in the car park, their breath clearly visible and ascending with the volumes of pungent smoke from the fireworks. Watching from the warmth and comfort of the lounge were half a dozen residents, their families and friends. Brian and Jill Hindmarsh were also there, making sure they spoke to each family. Even at this early hour several of the residents had already gone to bed.

The display lasted about half an hour and finished with a spectacular catherine wheel which sent out showers of golden sparks. Each child had been given sparklers, and these had been waved about with the usual excitement. And so finished another commemoration of the political strife of a former century between Roman Catholics and Protestants.

Trevor, armed with his bucket of sand and one of the home's fire extinguishers, was relieved that all had gone smoothly and safely. He was, with the elderly gardener, Frank, thanked by the spectators for 'doing the fireworks' and given a polite round of applause. Whilst the two of them cleared the rubbish away the rest of the folk made their way indoors.

'Gee, it's good to get indoors!'

'Nice show, though, nice show.'

'It's nice for the old folk, isn't it! They do enjoy this sort of thing, I always think.'

'Hello Mr Hindmarsh, how are you?'

'I'm well. Did your children enjoy the fireworks?'

'Mum, are there any burgers?'

'We'll see.'

'What did you think, Dave? Did you enjoy those?'

'Yes, I did enjoy those. Did you enjoy those?'

'Mum, are there any burgers left?'

'We'll see in a minute. Don't keep on!'

Back in the lounge, groups of adults stood chatting while their youngsters flicked through the TV channels. Several of the children were no strangers to the home. They either had an elderly relative who lived there, a parent who worked there or had visited the home with the school.

'Steve, are there any burgers left?'

* * * * * *

It may be a surprise to learn that Remembrance Sunday could have passed off unremembered as far as most of the residents were concerned. Only a few seemed occupied with memories of wartime, of battles fought, of comrades lost and of injuries sustained. All these were men. For these few it was a significant day, a day of remembering events that had occurred long ago but which seemed much more recent, events that never faded from the mind. In previous years the British Legion had left a tray of poppies and a collecting tin in the foyer. But this year things were different. Several visitors came in wearing poppies bought somewhere or other, but it was left for the staff to buy poppies for residents to wear.

Sunday saw the usual Remembrance Day service on the television. On the television in the first floor lounge, that is. Any BBC programmes had to be watched upstairs. Ted, Samuel, Henry, Ralph and Toby sat like the old comrades they were, united for a while by the service they had given for their country. They watched war veterans, the Royal Family and ever younger-looking politicians lay wreaths at the war memorial. They swapped stories about their days in the services and the action they had seen in various military campaigns. Each was aware that the others were not telling everything they had seen or experienced. They didn't have to. Each knew well enough what his friends were concealing.

* * * * * *

At the Golden Millennium Home for Elderly Travellers, one thing could be taken as certain. Each traveller who paused there for a few moments would bring with them the remainder of a long-ago-allotted span of days, months and years. The length of this remaining span remained confidential, and was never disclosed to the traveller.

QUIZ

Suggested answers are in italics.

'Night staff received requests for all sorts of things.'

57. What strange requests have you received from your residents during your night shifts?

• *Your answer.*

'Few residents seemed to be bothered about remembering the fifth of November and the gunpowder plot.'

58. Is there any point in trying to interest your residents in firework celebrations, the Queen's Jubilee celebrations or a royal wedding?

• *Your answer.*

My opinion is that there is. Celebrating such events helps to improve the quality of life for residents and enables them to keep in touch with everyday life. Families and friends are often willing to join in and provide practical support for any special event that the staff organise. **'Sunday saw the usual Remembrance Day service on the television.'**

59. What is the value in encouraging residents to wear poppies and to watch the Remembrance Day service on TV?

- *Your answer.*

- *Encourage your residents to concentrate on some of the positive aspects of remembering.*
- *The bravery of those who died.*
- *The freedom from oppression we have enjoyed in Britain due to the sacrifice of brave men and women.*
- *The tremendous community spirit that was often evident in those difficult days.*

My opinion is that as time passes fewer of our residents will have been involved in the Second World War, but an increasing number of them will have children and grandchildren who will have been killed or seriously injured in conflicts in Bosnia, Iran, Afghanistan, etc. These lost lives will also need to be remembered.

Printed in Great Britain
by Amazon.co.uk, Ltd.,
Marston Gate.